THE HUNTER'S PRAYER

ALSO BY KEVIN WIGNALL

Among the Dead

Dark Flag

People Die

Who Is Conrad Hirst?

KEVIN WIGNALL

THE HUNTER'S PRAYER

 THOMAS & MERCER

Text copyright © 2015 Kevin Wignall

Published by Thomas & Mercer, Seattle

www.apub.com

Amazon, the Amazon logo, and Thomas & Mercer are trademarks of Amazon.com, Inc., or its affiliates.

ISBN-13: 9781503946453
ISBN-10: 1503946452

Cover design by bürosüd° München, www.buerosued.de

Printed in the United States of America

For George S.
'Do you reject Satan?'

Part One

Chapter One

Seventeen-year-old boys die in car crashes. They die of meningitis, rare forms of cancer, suicide. Mostly, they don't die at all. They pass through the age, shedding awkwardness and anger and self-loathing on the way.

Ben Hatto was a seventeen-year-old close to bursting with anger. He was angry with his parents for stifling just about every plan he'd had for the summer ahead; angry with his sister, too, for spending the second successive summer traveling with someone from college; angry with school and life and everything else.

There was no teen awkwardness about him but he made up for it in self-loathing, centered at the moment on his hopeless infatuation with Alice Shaw, a girl completely out of his league, who thought of him as a friend if she thought of him at all. And today someone had asked him outright if he had a crush on her, and that's where he was now—one feeble, panicky denial away from total social humiliation.

He lay on his bed as the light faded, head propped up on a pillow, headphones with metal pounding, holding the world at bay. He'd eaten early—pasta. His parents had probably just finished their own dinner downstairs, hardly aware that he was even in the house with them.

His eyes were closed and he was thinking how he'd just have to ignore Alice completely through the final weeks of term. If one person suspected something, so would others and he'd become a laughing-stock. So he'd play it cool with her and over the summer he'd get his act together and then maybe it wouldn't seem so ridiculous that he liked someone that beautiful. Maybe.

It was something he could believe in for as long as he lay there— that he could be good-looking enough, cool enough, interesting enough for someone like her, that he could speak to her and say what he wanted to say, what he felt, and not the mess of words that actually came out. Lying there he could be everything he needed to be.

The trouble came when he left the security of his room, the posters, music, books, as though his personality was locked up in those familiar surroundings. He just wished for once that he could walk out of there, leave the house and not have everything fall apart, to be able to express himself, to be cool.

A track ended and in the two-second digital hush he heard his door open. He kept his eyes closed, let the next track explode into his ears, wanting whoever it was just to go away again. Then for one hopeful moment he imagined it being someone other than his parents—it was crazy, but if she were to come there, she might get to know him for who he really was, and then things might be different.

He opened his eyes. It wasn't one of his parents. It took him another second or two to take in the man standing there. Ben didn't know who it was and couldn't work out the expression on the stranger's face either: one of regret, or like someone about to break bad news.

Their eyes met. Confused, Ben reached up to take off the head-phones. The stranger lifted his arm swiftly at the same time, and the headphones were still in place, the music still pounding, when Ben felt something hit him hard on the head.

That was the last thing he felt, because Ben Hatto had just become a statistic in a subgroup almost entirely his own: seventeen-year-old boys killed in their own homes by professional hitmen.

The killer made his way back down the stairs, bypassing the kitchen where Pamela Hatto lay on the floor in front of the open dishwasher, her blood speckled across the freshly rinsed dishes she'd been stacking.

He passed through the hallway, stepping carefully over the pool of Mark Hatto's blood that had crept and expanded across the tile floor in the few minutes since he'd shot him. He eased the front door shut behind him, got back in his car and drove away.

The house he left was silent, the only noise the faint tinny racket of Ben's headphones, a false life-sign, like the lights that were already on here and there around the place. From the outside that's how it looked—like nothing was wrong, an affluent family home at peace on a summer's evening.

That affluence was visible, too, in the distance between the Hattos' house and those of their neighbors, the growing number of lights all isolated from each other in the lightly wooded garden landscape. This wealth was private, unobtrusive, the kind that would leave the deaths unnoticed for the night, the dead undisturbed.

But an earth tremor had taken place here, and however slowly, the shock waves would ripple out from the epicenter of the Hatto household, undermining the stability of people's lives at ever greater distances. It had already struck; they just didn't know it yet.

A few hundred yards away, their immediate neighbors were going about their own business, oblivious to the ghoulish adrenaline rush that would sweep them all up in the next twenty-four hours, beyond comprehending the legion of TV crews, journalists and photographers that would make the quiet neighborhood its own.

Further off, but still less than two miles away, the Shaw family was enjoying a barbecue with friends. Alice was there: happy, a little drunk on red wine, unaware that her feelings for Ben Hatto, confused as they were, would soon take on a lifelong significance, a mantle of sadness and regret and lost opportunity.

Five miles away in the nearest town, the CID unit had no idea they were about to have their first murder case in two years. Nor could they yet know who'd been living among them, or that within twenty-four hours they'd be announcing to the media that Mark Hatto's business affairs had been 'complex,' a shorthand way of telling the public not to worry, that this guy had brought it upon himself.

And thousands of miles away, in a small town in Italy, the place where the true force of the tremor would be measured, was a daughter, a sister, someone the police would need to contact to break the tragic news. And too late, it would be the detective who turned off Ben Hatto's music who'd puzzle over the boy's death and realize that perhaps his sister was also in danger. He'd stand there dwelling on the pointlessness of it, the fact that the kid clearly hadn't disturbed anyone, that the killer had known he was there, sought him out. And he alone would realize that this feud was total and that Ella Hatto, wherever she was, if she was still alive, was perhaps in as much danger as if she'd been in this house herself.

Chapter Two

They were people-watching, sitting on either side of the small table but with their chairs turned facing the street. There was plenty to look at—people sitting outside the other bars and cafes across the way, the *passaggiata* in full flow along this and the other main streets.

Every now and then Chris would point out someone in the crowd, a classic medallion man or a woman dressed like a hooker or transvestite, and they'd laugh about it. For the most part, though, they didn't talk, satisfied with watching, sipping at their drinks, winding down after the heat and hassle of the day.

The last few days had been hectic—Rome and Florence—but even so, Ella was pretty happy with the way things were going. Thailand with Susie the previous year had been a nightmare and a few people had warned her that traveling with a boyfriend was a classic recipe for a bad holiday and a wrecked relationship.

So far, though, things had gone well, and glad he was there with her. If she'd gone with anyone else, she'd have spent the whole time wishing Chris was with her anyway. She looked at him now, hair unkempt, his skin already tanned. He turned to meet her gaze, gave her a quizzical smile as he said, 'What?'

'Nothing.' She smiled and moved her head toward him. He leaned in for the kiss and gently pushed his tongue between her lips. She laughed a little and kissed him back for a few seconds before becoming self-conscious and breaking away.

'Later,' she said, facing back into the street, 'without the audience.' She scanned the crowd, reassuring herself that no one had been looking anyway.

'You're so Anglo-Saxon,' said Chris, joking.

'And you're such an Italian stallion.'

'Oh yeah. Trust me, before the night's out I'm getting a medallion and a chest wig.'

She laughed and they went back to watching. Her eyes were snagged immediately by a man sitting at the cafe directly across from them. He didn't look Italian but apart from that he was nondescript, average-looking, a guy in his forties maybe: short hair, medium build, a face and look that seemed designed to be lost in a crowd.

And that was the intriguing part, because she'd singled him out and, now that she was looking at him, Ella was certain she'd seen him before. She closed her eyes momentarily but couldn't picture him like that and had to open them again to remind herself what he looked like.

He seemed to be studying the *passaggiata* so she took the opportunity to study him in turn, staring at him as she tried to recall where she might have seen him. Maybe it had been in the railway station in Rome, or on the Ponte Vecchio perhaps, or the Duomo.

She became uneasy at the possibility of him having been in Rome *and* Florence, in all of those places, and after trying to shake the thought for a while she said, 'Chris, see the guy sitting across from us, short-sleeved blue shirt, forties?'

'What about him?'

'I know it sounds weird but I'm pretty certain he was in Rome and Florence.'

'So who do you think he's stalking—you or me?' She laughed. 'Look, somewhere like Italy, everyone goes the same places. There's probably loads of people here who were in Rome and Florence.'

He was exaggerating, ignoring the fact that this was hardly one of the most obvious stops on the tour of Italy. And yet he was probably still right; in Thailand last year she and Susie had kept bumping into the same people as they'd traveled around the country, some of them in the most unlikely places.

She looked at the man again, annoyed that it was troubling her, finally making an effort to dismiss it altogether.

'It's nice here, isn't it? More relaxed.'

'Doesn't seem as hot either. Maybe we should stay here a few days, take in one of the spas, chill out.'

'Suits me,' she said. 'Venice can wait.' She looked back across the street. It took her a moment or two to pick him out again and when she spotted him she noticed he was looking agitated, an edginess that rubbed off on her. He was looking up the street, and she looked in the same direction, unable to see anything, nobody standing out from the crowd.

She glanced back and jumped nervously. He was staring directly at her now, getting out of his seat. She began to panic, thoughts crashing into each other. A group of kids walked in front of her and by the time they'd passed he was halfway across the street and looking up it again.

He was reaching under his shirt for something as he walked and then it was there in his hand: a gun. This couldn't be happening. This guy had been following them, she knew it, and now he was heading towards them with a gun. Her heart stalled and for a second she couldn't speak. The words finally burst out.

'Shit! Chris!' She didn't have time to say any more. She heard Chris respond but couldn't make out what he'd said. The man was almost on top of her and then she heard the gunshots, deafening, followed by screams, shouts, panic.

He was standing in front of her, his back to her. He'd fired two shots, and a few yards away in the street two men had fallen. He looked around quickly, took two steps forward, aimed at the head of one of the men and fired again. Another shocked chorus from the crowd.

Ella heard Chris again, some garbled expletive, and the man was back with them, his face close, no longer edgy but calm and authoritative.

'Come with me.'

Ella got to her feet but heard Chris saying, 'No fucking way.'

'Come with me or I'll kill you right now.' He was pointing the gun at him.

'Do what he says, Chris.'

They were walking quickly now through the panicked street and it took her a while to notice that the gunman was leading her by the arm. They were all mute, a tight ball of silence moving swiftly away from the chaos behind them. She looked at Chris a couple of times but he wasn't taking anything in, lost in the shock and confusion of the moment.

They'd just seen two people killed and now they were walking away with the killer, a man who'd threatened Chris too, and yet they were going quietly, unquestioning, putting up no resistance. They were all moving with a shared sense of urgency because somehow in the time-lapse nightmare of the last few minutes it had seemed like he was protecting them.

'You get in the passenger seat. Ella, in the back. Lie down.' They got into the car he'd led them to and Ella lay down as he drove away, the movement of the car adding an extra layer of disorientation to the mix. She could hear sirens now, and this man knew her name.

'What the *fuck* is going on?' It was Chris, his voice too loud, burning off the adrenaline. 'And who the fuck are you? And what . . . Just . . . What's going on? Fuck!'

At first it seemed like he wouldn't answer but after a brief pause he spoke, his voice still calm and low, sounding subdued after Chris's shock-fueled rant.

'Probably an attempted kidnap. I'm Lucas. Mark Hatto asked me to watch Ella in case of something like this.'

'So I did see you in Rome and Florence.'

'You can get up now.' She sat up. They were away from the town and it was darker.

'Where are we going?'

'Florence for tonight. I'll call your dad from there.'

Chris turned in his seat and looked at her, his features shadowy and indistinct. 'Why would someone wanna kidnap you?'

'I don't know.'

'And a bodyguard?' His tone was accusatory. 'I mean, what the hell is that all about?'

'I don't know, Chris! I don't fucking know, okay?'

'Okay! Jesus!' He turned forward again but after a few seconds he said to Lucas, 'What about you? Care to enlighten us?'

'They're rich.' It sounded like he'd go on to say something else but he didn't and in waiting for him to finish they fell into silence by default.

Ella tried to think back to the scene in Montecatini, putting it back together in her head, trying to make sense of it. Lucas had looked agitated and he'd been looking up the street in the direction the two men had come from. The way he'd stood in front of her too—surely that's what a bodyguard would have done.

She still couldn't process the fact that two men were dead, or the measured way Lucas had shot one of them in the head after he'd fallen. That hadn't been defense or protection: that had been an execution. And she still couldn't process that she was at the center of this, that she needed to be watched, that there were people out there who might want to kidnap her.

Why her? They weren't rich. They were well-off, comfortable, but it wasn't like her dad ever made the rich list or anything. That meant there were at least a thousand people in the country who were richer than they were, a thousand people with daughters or sons or grandchildren worth much more to a kidnapper than she was. So why her?

'Did you follow me in Thailand last year?'

'No.'

'Did anyone?'

'I don't know.'

Chris turned to him and said, 'What about at college?' The question annoyed her, Chris sounding more concerned about his own privacy being breached than he was about her safety or what had just happened. Maybe he was right to be concerned, but it annoyed her all the same.

'I don't know,' said Lucas, as if he, too, was irritated by the questions. 'I was just asked to keep an eye on you in Europe, that's all.'

He slowed and pulled over next to a phone booth. There was a small supermarket across the road, a garage fifty yards away, lit like stage sets under the deep black of the sky.

'Stay in the car.' He got out and walked over to the phone. They couldn't hear him talking but he kept looking at them all the time he spoke.

'He took the keys,' said Chris. 'For someone who's meant to be on our side, he doesn't seem to trust us much.'

'Check the glove compartment.'

'What for?'

'I don't know. ID or something.' Chris reached down casually and checked but found nothing.

'It's a rental car.'

A scooter approached at speed from behind, the sudden high-pitched drone startling her. It sped past them, two good-looking Italian boys, the wind pulling at their hair and their shirts, giving them an air of sleekness and freedom.

The one sitting on the back was laughing and had turned briefly and looked at the car as they'd passed. For a second Ella felt like he'd looked at her, the smile for her, his eyes inviting.

And now they'd disappeared and she was envious—of their open road, of their carefree night, a night that had been hers too just half an hour before, though she hadn't appreciated it then. Maybe she would have if she'd known how soon it would end.

'I need to call my dad. Have you got your phone?'

'Yeah.' He handed the phone back to her. She held it close to the window to pick up some of the streetlight but before she could start dialing she noticed that Lucas had seen her and that he looked in a hurry to end his call. Within seconds he was back at the car, opening the door.

'Turn it off.'

'I was calling my dad.'

'Not on that. Turn it off. I'll call your dad when we get to Florence.' She turned off the phone and handed it back to Chris. Lucas shut the door again and got back in the driver's seat. He turned to face them both. 'Keep your phones switched off. Don't be tempted to make a call, don't be tempted to use your credit cards, do nothing to give away your identity or location, not until we know what's going on.'

Chris said, 'What about you? Who were you calling?'

'Hotel in Florence.' He started the car and pulled away. 'It's high season. Best to book ahead.' They didn't respond and a moment later he said, 'That was a little joke there. Just trying to lighten the mood.'

Chris threw him a look of contempt and said, 'After what we just saw you do, you expect us to laugh at your standup routine? When do you get to the jokes about shooting people?'

Lucas glanced across at him and said, 'What did you see me do? Tell me. What did you see me do?' His voice was threatening and Chris didn't answer.

Maybe he'd saved them, but Ella couldn't shake the memory of what she had seen: Lucas taking a step forward, shooting the man in the head. Treading carefully with her tone, she said, 'Lucas?' She caught his eyes in the rear-view and felt confident enough to proceed. 'Why did you shoot him in the head?'

'He was wearing body armor.'

'How do you know?'

'Because he didn't bleed enough when I shot him.' Again, it sounded like he'd go on to say something else but he didn't. He seemed to have a way with awkward conversation-ending pauses and none of them spoke for the rest of the journey.

It was after ten by the time they got to Florence, the traffic still fairly heavy and volatile, crowds of people spilling across the streets. They'd been among them the night before, and probably so had Lucas, a realization that left her feeling violated, betrayed.

Lucas parked up in a side street and told them to get out, then opened the trunk. Inside were a large backpack and an overnight bag. He gave the backpack to Chris and reached into the other bag.

'Take these.' He handed them a passport each. 'False passports, for the hotel. Okay, let's go.' He picked up the bag, locked the car and led them along the street, clearly sensing they were still in danger.

They'd walked a good twenty paces before Ella thought of looking at the passport in her hand, bearing her picture but with the name 'Emma Wright.' Chris showed her his open passport. She couldn't see the name but it was his picture, too.

It was a relief to get to the hotel and off the crowded streets. This was no longer a friendly place, the people no longer just tourists. The hotel was on the fourth floor of a building near the Duomo, a budget hotel but clean, the rooms en suite. It was a lot better than the one they'd booked for themselves.

Lucas introduced himself as Mr. Wright. He'd booked two rooms but once the manager had left them in the corridor he said, 'We all stay in the double.' They didn't respond, just followed him into the room.

Chris dropped the backpack on the bed and Lucas immediately unfastened it and took out a gun, then something else that he attached to the barrel—a silencer. His movements were spare and methodical, but somehow he looked unpredictable, dangerous.

Ella felt her stomach tighten: maybe Lucas had set a trap and here they were in it. But with the gun assembled he turned to Chris and said, 'I have to go out. I won't be long. When I get back, I'll knock once and say, "It's Dad here." Anyone else knocks, don't answer. Anyone comes in, you shoot them. Safety's off. Just aim it at the middle of their chest and shoot. If you're in any doubt, shoot again, keep shooting till they go down, and then shoot them in the head.'

Ella said, 'You don't think we're still in danger?'

He turned to her and smiled, his face coming alive, taking on form, becoming warm, friendly. His eyes were pale blue, startlingly blue, something she hadn't noticed before. 'No. It's just a precaution.' He turned back to Chris. 'Okay, you understand what I'm saying? You want to hold the gun to get used to it?' Chris shook his head, looking lost, like a child. 'I'll put it here on the table.' He walked to the door, but stopped before leaving and said, 'And remember, no phone calls, no nothing.'

That was it—he was gone, and the two of them were left standing in the confined hush of the room. It was as if, for the first time since it had happened, they suddenly had the space and the quiet to take it all in. Ella wanted to cry now and for Chris to hold her but he still looked lost, distracted.

'I need a piss,' he said, as though becoming aware of his own body again. He went into the bathroom and shut the door. Ella sat down on the edge of the bed and looked at the gun, sitting there on the night table like it was the most natural thing in the world. She didn't want to cry now; she just wanted Lucas to come back.

Chris was a long time in the bathroom and when he came out his eyes were red. She'd never seen him cry, had never even seen him upset, and she wanted to hold him and comfort him the way she'd wanted to be comforted a few minutes before. He looked embarrassed, though, and laced with hostility, an anger she couldn't help but feel was directed at her.

'Are you okay?'

He didn't answer, saying instead, 'How do we know who this guy is? I mean, how do we really know what's going on here? You never told me your family was this rich.'

'They're not.'

He shrugged, as if that proved his point.

'And yet you're willing to believe this guy's being paid by your father to act as a bodyguard, protect you against kidnappers. How do we even know those two guys were kidnappers?'

'They had guns.' Though now that she thought about it, she couldn't remember seeing guns.

'So? Maybe they were the police. That would explain the body armor. Because why would a kidnapper wear body armor? What, he thought you might be packing a gun?' It troubled her but he had a point. They didn't know anything about Lucas, if that was his real name, and they had only his word for it that he'd been paid to protect them, to protect her. 'For all we know, he could be out there calling your dad right now and demanding a ransom. What a classic trick for a kidnapper—you convince your victims they're in danger and that you're protecting them.'

She thought about it, all the question marks, the apparent unwillingness of Lucas to provide answers for any of them. The sum of their knowledge was that Lucas had been following them, that he'd killed two men without hesitation, that he had false passports with their pictures in them. All the same, he had an air about him of someone who was being straight with them.

'I believe him,' she said finally. 'If he was lying he'd have tried to convince us, but he hasn't. He just assumes we believe him because he's telling the truth and he can't see why we wouldn't believe. I know this is all crazy and, trust me, I really wanna speak to my dad, but I think Lucas is telling the truth.'

Chris looked at her, not saying anything. He nodded then, seeming to accept that she was probably right, and he looked down at the gun and said, 'Then we're in some really deep shit.'

Ella looked at the gun too, but in her head she was silently correcting him; *they* weren't in really deep shit, *she* was. Whatever this was, sooner or later Chris would be able to walk away from it if he wanted to, and from her.

She had an uneasy feeling, though, that sitting on that night table was a reality she'd been shielded from, a reality that her father hadn't wanted to taint her childhood or youth. But it had surfaced now and even if she came through this, if nothing ever happened again, she'd be forever on her guard, always scanning the crowd for another Lucas.

Chapter Three

Lucas had a feeling something was wrong. He'd called twice, allowing for the fact that the first call might have woken them up, that Hatto might not have reached the phone in time. Both calls had run onto the answering machine, though. He'd try again in the morning, but he didn't like this at all.

He started towards the hotel, unsure if he could face going back just yet. In five days watching these kids he'd come to like them, even envy them—youth, young love, all that. But it was easy to like people from a distance; being cooped up with them was another thing.

They probably needed some time on their own anyway, and he couldn't imagine they were in that much danger, not for the time being. He'd stay out for half an hour, have a drink and then go back. Maybe if he was lucky, they'd be tired by then.

He walked into the Duomo square and headed for an Irish bar with a small fenced terrace outside, just enough cramped stools and tables for a dozen or so people. Only three people were sitting there, so he went into the more crowded bar, bought a glass of red and came back out.

The group of three looked at him as he sat down but went back to their conversation. Italians, intellectual types. He listened in to the rhythm of their speech for a while before letting it fall away into the murmur coming from the bar itself.

Tourists were still walking about the piazza but most of them were quiet, necks uncraned, as if in the cool darkness they'd forgotten where they were. The cathedral looked at peace too, sheer above them, an air of respite about it. This was how Lucas liked cities.

He wished he'd brought his book with him. He only had about fifty pages left and could have finished it, enjoying the calm, his glass of red wine. It would have looked obvious, though, leaving them on urgent business but stopping to pick up some reading matter on the way out. And as it happened, he wouldn't have read much anyway.

He'd only been there ten minutes when a mixed group of five or six arrived, English and Americans. They were in high spirits, not drunk but loud and happy, spilling onto the terrace with a force that looked set to sweep the three intellectuals away. After a few moments of guarded contempt, though, the Italians went back to their conversation.

Lucas continued to mind his own business and when one of the American girls asked if she could take a spare stool from his table he smiled and gestured for her to take it but said nothing, not wanting to be drawn out as an English speaker.

One of the group had gone into the bar and came out a short while later with a tray of drinks. He was clowning around, walking out into the empty square like a confused waiter. They called him back, but he kept it up, pretending to offer Lucas one of the drinks, cracking jokes.

This guy was clearly the reason they were in such high spirits. He was pretty funny too, but Lucas was in no mood. He finished his drink and edged past them off the terrace. He heard one of the girls say, 'You scared him off.'

The clown responded with a plaintive child voice.

'Oh, don't go.'

Ten years ago Lucas would have stayed calm by thinking of the power he had, knowing that he could pull his gun at any second and hold it against the guy's head—*Not so funny now, huh?* He'd changed since then. He couldn't imagine he'd ever want to join in with the fun but he was more Zen now, consoling himself with the thought that one day, all these people would be dead.

When he got back to the room, he listened outside the door for a minute. They were talking, their voices hushed but urgent, no doubt still debating what had gone on, whether or not they could trust Lucas. He knocked once, silencing them, a silence that was somehow more frantic than the conversation that had preceded it.

'It's Dad here.'

'Coming,' said Ella after a pause, her tone falsely cheerful. She let him in. Chris was standing on the far side of the bed and Lucas noticed immediately that he was empty-handed. He glanced at the bedside table, then at Ella, relieved as he saw the gun in her hand, hanging at her side. She'd gone for the gun; that was good.

Once she'd closed the door she put it back on the table and said, 'Where have you been?'

'I tried to call your dad. No reply. I'll try again in the morning.'

Chris looked at his watch and said, 'Maybe they're in bed.' He was still standing in the same place, like someone in a wooden amateur theater production, uneasy in his own space.

Lucas nodded but Ella said quickly, 'Ben wouldn't be in bed.' She shrugged then, answering herself. 'He doesn't always pick up the phone, though.'

Lucas looked at her, thought of saying something and decided against it, turning on the TV instead. He went through a couple of channels—soccer, a hallucinatory game show—stopping on something that looked like the news.

As he watched, he was conscious of the two of them behind him. Chris was static, like he wasn't sure who had the next line, an air of suppressed panic at the thought it might be him. Ella seemed more relaxed, projecting a slightly bewildered acceptance.

Out of the corner of his eye he saw her sit on the foot of the bed, watching with him now. They were covering a political story, pictures of Berlusconi, other people he didn't recognize.

When that story finished, the anchor spoke for a minute or two and all three of them heard him mention Montecatini. It kicked Chris back into life, bringing him over to sit next to Ella. There was some footage of the aftermath, a confused crowd, police, a covered body on the ground.

The last thing the camera fixed on was a gun that had been dropped by one of them. It lay in the road now, a MAC-10. That's how Lucas had spotted them so quickly; if they'd been carrying something more discreet they might just have slipped a couple of shots in before he got to them.

And that was something else the MAC-10 said to him, something he wouldn't share with Ella—that this hadn't been an attempted kidnap: it had been a hit. He didn't know what kind of business Hatto was involved in now but he had to have upset someone in a big way for them to consider this a reasonable payback.

A policeman was being interviewed, talking rapidly with a look of grave concern that didn't match the excited flow of words coming from his mouth. Lucas was staring intently at the screen, just staring—it hadn't occurred to him to wonder what was being said. But then Ella said, 'What is it? What's he saying?'

He turned and shrugged.

'I only speak English.'

She smiled a little. 'You don't speak much of that.'

He nodded, smiled back. He wanted to say something but couldn't think of a response. He wasn't much good at conversation, he knew that; never able to come up with the mindless chitchat people used to fill the pauses.

'Will the police be looking for us?' It was Chris, still shocked, taking too long to snap out of it.

'Me. Maybe you.'

Chris looked confused for a second before saying, 'Why don't we just go to the police?'

Lucas shook his head. 'Not until I know what's going on.'

'So what are we gonna do?'

'You should sleep. Tomorrow might be a tough day.' He could see from their faces what they were thinking, that it could hardly be tougher than the last couple of hours.

It could, though, and Lucas was uncomfortable with the thought of what might still lie ahead of them. He didn't know how to deal with people who were falling apart, how to comfort them. He wasn't sure if he'd just forgotten how to be with people at all.

He turned off the TV and sat down in the small armchair in the corner of the room—a token gesture by the owners to mimic bigger, better hotels. Ella looked at him for a moment or two and said, 'We haven't got our things.'

'I know.' It was funny how people fixed on little things—the lack of a toothbrush and a change of underwear seemingly more important than the fact that two gunmen had tried to kidnap or kill them. 'It's only for one night.'

'Do you at least have some toothpaste I could borrow?'

'Sure.' He went over to his bag, took the toothpaste out and handed it to her.

'Thanks.' She walked into the bathroom and Lucas took his book out before going back to the armchair.

Chris was still on the end of the bed. He took his shoes off, a laborious process, like he'd aged fifty years. Lucas ignored him and turned his attention to the book, rereading the last couple of pages to get himself back into the story.

And he tried to keep his eyes on the book when Ella came out of the bathroom, stripped down to her underwear, carrying her clothes neatly folded. He couldn't help but be drawn, though, to the backs of her thighs, the slimly drawn curves of her hips and waist, the skimpy tease of the matching black underwear.

She put the clothes near the bed, wrestling under the duvet before tossing the remaining items on the pile. Lucas looked at them, the material flimsy and spent, even more suggestive of the nakedness that was tantalizingly out of reach beneath the duvet.

Perhaps Chris had noticed him looking because he stood up now, staring at Ella like he was mystified by something, probably just by the fact she'd been happy to walk around like that in front of a stranger. He started to put his shoes back on.

Lucas put the book down and said, 'What are you doing?'

He finished tying his laces, then stared at Lucas defiantly.

'I need some fresh air. I'm going out.'

Ella lifted her head and stared at Lucas too, waiting for his response. Chris looked wired, determined to get out of there for a while, certainly in no mood to listen to reason. Lucas was hoping Ella might say something, plead with him to stay, but she remained silent, probably sensing, as he did, that it was pointless.

There were other ways of stopping him, of course, but he supposed they were hardly appropriate for a situation like this. The simple truth was, he should never have agreed to the job in the first place; it wasn't what he specialized in, protecting people, baby-sitting.

But here he was, shark playing dolphin, jumping through the hoops but fooling no one.

'Give me your phone.'

Chris reached into his pocket and threw the phone on the bed, a petty act that seemed to embarrass him once he'd done it. He looked earnestly at Lucas and said, 'I won't be long. I just need some space, you know? Fresh air.'

Lucas nodded. 'Don't do anything stupid. Don't call anyone, don't speak to anyone. When you get back, you knock once and say, "It's Craig."'

'Okay.' He turned to Ella and said, 'You'll be okay?'

She let her head sink back to the pillow and said, 'I'll be fine but, like he said, Chris, don't do anything stupid.'

He left without answering, and Lucas got up and locked the door behind him. As he sat down again, he heard Ella say, 'Sorry about Chris.' He looked over. He was about to tell her it was okay, to forget about it, but realized it wasn't what she needed to hear.

'How are you holding up?'

'Not well.' She sat up, propping the pillows behind her, all the time careful to keep herself covered with the duvet. She looked set to say something, but once she was comfortable she noticed the book in his hand and said, 'What are you reading?'

'*The Nibelungenlied.*'

'The what?'

'It's an old German epic poem, the story Wagner used for the Ring Cycle. Of course, the opera isn't as good as the book.' She didn't even smile, but that was hardly surprising; she was worried and upset, and he spent too much time on his own, his sense of humor stuck in a cul-de-sac where it was required to amuse only him.

'You read that stuff for pleasure?'

'It's a good story.'

She shrugged and said, 'Did you go to college?' He shook his head. She thought for a second or two before saying, 'Have you read any Jane Austen?'

He shook his head again.

'Never thought it was my kind of thing.'

'You should try *Persuasion*. I just finished it. I'd lend you my copy but it's in my bag.' He smiled. He liked that they were discussing books, like a real conversation. It wasn't real, obviously, but it felt close, to him at least.

'You should try this, too,' he said. Her mind was already elsewhere, though, probably dragged back by the thought of her bag sitting in their hotel room in Montecatini. It wasn't a conversation, and her mind wouldn't allow her the luxury of talking books when there were more important things.

She looked deep in thought for a while before saying, 'Do you really think they were trying to kidnap me?' It took him a moment to register the tone of the question; she wasn't searching for a more innocent interpretation but for a darker one. It made him think she'd had more idea of her father's business interests than Hatto had given her credit for.

'It's hard to say. There are a lot of enthusiastic amateurs out there at the moment. They don't always act like you expect them to.'

'But?'

'My guess is they were sent to kill you.'

She didn't respond, and then she started to gag and ran for the bathroom, clutching the duvet but not managing to cover herself with it.

Lucas took in the flash of exposed flesh, the glimpse of pubic hair, the details searing into his memory before she was gone. He listened in shock as she threw up into the toilet. It didn't last long but it was another five minutes before she came out. The duvet was more securely wrapped now, only her head and feet exposed.

She sat on the edge of the bed and Lucas said, 'I'm sorry. I wouldn't have said anything. I had the feeling maybe you knew.'

Ella shook her head before saying, 'I always thought Dad's businesses were . . .' She stopped herself. 'I always thought there were things we were never told. But even so, why would someone want to kill *me*?'

'I don't know; maybe to get at him.' He thought of reassuring her about Hatto's business activities too, how it was mainly finance now, and legitimate on the whole. He couldn't be certain, though; his own assurances were based on incomplete information, and on just one source: Hatto himself. 'This is something you'll have to speak to your dad about.'

'We should call him now.'

'I tried. There was no answer.'

'So we keep trying until we wake them up.'

'What good would that do? We'll try again in the morning.'

'And what if they're in danger too?' He wanted to tell her what he was really thinking, what his gut had told him the second time Hatto had failed to pick up the phone, but he knew this time to keep his mouth shut. If he was right, then he was only putting off the inevitable. But hopefully, by the time the devastation hit he'd have already passed her into the comforting hands of an embassy or consulate.

'Your dad hired me to watch you. You really think he needs advice on security?' He smiled, an attempt to show her there was nothing to worry about. 'Now I need you to stay calm. I don't know if we're out of the woods yet and Chris is losing it. I need you to be cool, even if you don't feel it.'

She nodded and said, 'You think he's okay?'

She was talking about Chris, and there it was all over her face, how much she was in love with him. The truth was, Lucas didn't really care whether Chris was okay or not, only that he didn't blow their cover. He was pretty certain, too, that someone who did this kind of thing professionally wouldn't have let him walk out that door.

'It's a safe city; he needed some air. Maybe it'll help him pull himself together.'

'You know, he isn't usually like this; he's a really great person.'

'I know.' He didn't bother reminding her that he'd been watching them for almost a week and had a good idea what both of them were like, in their own world if not in this rewritten one. 'And anyway, what does it matter what I think of either of you?'

She nodded a little. It didn't matter what he thought; he was nobody, a man cut off from life, even cut off from the life that had been his own, brought in again only by this favor he'd not been obliged to grant. And he wished he hadn't granted it but he'd still see it through, get her to safety, even back to Hatto if he was still alive.

'You should try to sleep,' he said. She looked hopefully at the door before shuffling back up the bed and releasing her grip on the duvet. A few seconds later she turned on her side, away from him. He had the feeling she was still awake, waiting for Chris, but after a short while he opened his book again, immersing himself in its distant armor-clad battles.

He was sitting there with the finished book on his lap when he heard the door at the end of the corridor open and close, and then clumsy footsteps. Ella lifted her head up off the pillow before Chris reached the door. The knock came and the stumbling, self-correcting words, 'It's Chri . . . It's Craig here.' Lucas opened the door and let him in.

As Lucas locked the door, he heard Ella say, 'How are you feeling?'

'Okay. What about you?'

'I was worried about you.'

'Sorry.' He turned to face Lucas and said, 'I had a few beers.'

It was something he didn't need to tell either of them but Lucas said, 'It's okay. Get some sleep.'

'I need a piss first.' He walked heavily into the bathroom and Lucas exchanged a smile with Ella.

At least with the few beers Chris might sleep now, and if he slept, he'd be more likely to deal with whatever came tomorrow. Ella was different; even with what had happened earlier, he was confident enough she'd cope with whatever came her way. She had that look about her, of someone who didn't know the beginnings of how tough she could be.

Chris came out of the bathroom, made an attempt to remove some of his clothes and crashed onto the bed. Ella smoothed his hair and responded in kind to his sloppy embrace. They became almost instantly still and quiet so Lucas turned off the light and sat back in his chair, staring out across the dark room.

He tried to think back to the book but the feeling had already gone. Instead, he could think only of the job at hand. In theory, the most difficult part was already behind him: he'd kept her alive, unharmed. In the morning he'd set about getting her to safety.

If Mark Hatto picked up the phone in the morning it wouldn't be a problem, just a question of logistics. But if Hatto was dead, then the guys sent after Ella had been part of something much bigger, a hit complex and organized enough to leave Lucas out of his depth, particularly after a couple of years in retirement.

Nobody would be scared of him anymore, or of his reputation. Some of these young punks probably didn't know he'd ever existed.

She didn't know it as she lay there sleeping, but probably the best thing Ella had going for her at the moment was the fact that no one considered him a threat anymore, that no one considered him much at all.

Chapter Four

He'd waited a couple of minutes since the first call but again, it ran onto the answering machine. He looked at his watch but it didn't matter what the time was here, there or anywhere else. No one was answering the phone in the Hatto house and Lucas didn't want to know why because he didn't want to have to tell her. He wanted someone else to break the news.

He walked back to the car. The sun was fierce so he kept to the side of the street still in shadow and pressed through the tourists. He took the car back and bought tickets for the ten o'clock train. If he was handing them over, the consulate in Zurich was as good a place as any. And if it got messier, then at least he'd be playing on his home turf.

He started back to the hotel, stopping on the way to buy a duffel bag and a large backpack and toiletries. A part of him was thinking that he was going to too much trouble, that he'd be better off sending them to the police here in Florence.

And if Hatto was dead he wouldn't even get the rest of the money. Here he was, though, determined to get her back alive, and he knew it was nothing to do with compassion, just a perverse professional pride, like a lawyer determined to win every case, no matter who the defendant was.

Lucas had the key but when he got back he could hear them talking so he knocked. 'It's Dad here.' Chris opened the door. They were both dressed but looked full of sleep, unkempt. Neither of them had gone for the gun this time.

He threw the things on the bed and said, 'Toothbrushes and stuff. Freshen up; we're going out.'

'Where?'

'There's a department store nearby. We'll buy you both some clothes to put in these bags. Then we're getting a train out of here.'

Ella looked troubled, confused, as she said, 'I don't get it. I thought you were gonna call Dad today and we'd get a plane home.'

Lucas looked at his watch, a feint, luring her away from the truth she might see buried in his eyes.

'I'll call him from Milan when we're changing trains. I want to get away from here.'

Chris seemed edgy now and said, 'So where are you taking us?'

'Switzerland.' He handed Ella the bag of toiletries and said, 'And remember, when we're out, call me Dad.'

Ella smiled in response and said, 'You know, you don't actually look old enough to be our father.'

'So don't call me anything. Just don't call me Lucas, not in front of other people.' Her smile dropped and he realized too late that she'd paid him a compliment, that she'd tried to be nice to him and that it might have been more appropriate to thank her, maybe say something nice in return.

Their mood lightened when they got to the department store, joking with each other as they shopped. And when Lucas paid, Ella smiled broadly at him and said, 'Thanks, Dad.'

'Yeah, thanks, Dad.'

He looked at them and smiled a little.

'You're welcome.' He tried to smile at the girl behind the counter, but she was surly in response. She could tell, he thought, that whatever was going on here, he was no father, and not because he looked too young.

It was good to see Chris loosening up. He kept joking with Ella as they walked back to the hotel with the bags of clothes. Her good spirits were unlikely to make it through the day but Lucas reckoned on finding it easier if Chris was together enough to comfort her when the time came.

Lucas was still scanning the crowd as they walked. There seemed to be only tourists on the streets but he'd be glad to get out of Florence; he knew too well, from his own experience that tourist cities were easy places to kill someone.

When they got back, he kept it up, stepping into the lobby and glancing around before letting them pass. He looked quickly back out into the street then as Ella and Chris made towards the elevator. And then he heard her name spoken behind him, and it wasn't Chris's voice but somebody European.

'Ella.' A false cheerfulness, like an old friend unexpectedly encountered.

Lucas spun around, reaching under his shirt for his gun. Where had he come from? Behind the stairs, maybe. He should have seen him and now it was too late. Ella turned at the sound of her name and the guy was right there, lifting his gun to her face.

Chris was at the elevator door, staring back in shock. Ella still had the quizzical look she'd worn on turning. Lucas could feel his own painfully slow movements, the gun seeming to snag as he pulled it free, and the other guy ready to shoot.

And then, as Lucas continued to move, something strange happened. For a second, a second only, the other three appeared to freeze, Chris with his static look of terror, Ella unable to shift away from that puzzled smile, and the gunman, his finger on the trigger but not squeezing, the tip of the silencer just a few inches away from her face.

Lucas couldn't see his face properly, only the side of his head, and then there was his own hand and gun in a line with it, like someone else had put it there for him. He pulled the trigger and the guy dropped, the roar of the gun echoing through the lobby like a slammed door.

He moved quickly now, pushing Ella and Chris into the elevator, taking the guy's gun and handing it to Ella. He looked around the lobby again before dragging the body into the shadows behind the first flight of stairs. There was blood everywhere but the lobby was gloomy so maybe no one would notice for a while.

He got into the elevator with them and pressed the fourth-floor button. They were both staring at him, shell-shocked, though he guessed that was better than having them panicked and screaming.

Ella's face and top were bloodied, flecks of it sticky in her hair. He wiped the worst of it from her face with his fingers and then he prised the gun out of her hand and dropped it into one of the bags.

'When we walk past reception, you walk on this side of me, okay?' He was looking directly into her eyes and got a twitching nod back in response. 'Chris, you okay?' Another uncertain nod. 'Good. Just hold it together till we get back to the room.'

The reception area was empty, but Lucas kept them tight, covering the angles as they made towards the room, hoping that the guy downstairs had been on his own. And he was still angry with himself because if the shooter hadn't hesitated it would have been job over. He should have seen him, should have been more vigilant.

Once in the room Lucas locked the door behind him and checked that the bathroom was clear. Ella was gasping for air, like she'd been underwater since entering the lobby and had only just surfaced. He took hold of her by the shoulders and said, 'You okay?' She nodded, tears running into the blood on her cheeks, but he could tell she was fighting now, regrouping.

'It's my fault.' Lucas turned and looked at Chris. He was standing in the corner, timid. 'It's my fault,' he said again.

'You called someone, didn't you?'

'From a phone booth,' he said defensively. 'And I only called home. I spoke to my brother.'

'And told him what?'

'Where we were. The hotel.' He looked scared, and maybe with good reason. Lucas could feel himself coiling up with anger.

'You stupid fuck.'

'I didn't know whether I could trust you. I wanted someone to know where we were, in case . . .'

'In case what?' He didn't answer. 'In case what? Because good for you, you let someone know where we were.' He was moving towards him, the anger swelling, breaking. Ella made some desperate plea for calm but all Lucas could see was Chris and the fact he'd nearly got her killed.

'I'm sorry, I didn't . . .' Lucas grabbed him by the shirt and threw him. Chris stumbled and fell onto the edge of the bed. He grabbed him again and put the gun between his eyes.

'This close! *This close!* You stupid fuck!'

Chris was crying now, pleading incomprehensibly, and he could hear Ella saying, 'Please, Lucas, don't. Lucas, don't,' and then he could smell urine and Chris's features crumpled further into humiliation. Suddenly all he could see was the boy he was standing over and he felt sick for what he'd just done to him, in front of his girlfriend.

'I'm sorry,' he said, and stepped back.

Chris sank down onto the floor and said, 'Bastard.'

'I know, I'm sorry. I was angry.' He wasn't sure if Ella had seen the wet patch on Chris's trousers so he said, 'Look, we don't have a lot of time. Ella, go into the bathroom, change your clothes, wash your face, get the blood out of your hair.' She looked at him like she needed reassurance, maybe that it was over, that he wouldn't do anything more to Chris. 'It's okay. Go on.'

She went into the bathroom, still clutching the shopping bags she'd been carrying. With the door closed, Lucas said, 'I don't think she noticed. Change your clothes, bag them and toss them.' Chris didn't move at first so he added, 'You know, there's no shame in what just happened. I've known some pretty tough guys do the same thing, and worse.'

Chris looked up at him with contempt and said, 'Don't fucking patronize me.' He got up and pulled some clothes out of a bag.

'Okay, and I am sorry. I was just angry. I mean, Jesus, don't you watch movies?'

'Yes, I do.' He looked angry himself, and wronged, as he said, 'You told us it was an attempted kidnap. I don't know what the fuck's going on, I don't even know if you do, but kidnappers don't tap the telephone of the victim's boyfriend's family. And that man you killed downstairs—he didn't look like he wanted to kidnap her at all.' Lucas felt uneasy, sensing that Chris was close to guessing how out of his depth he was, and how unsuited to protection work.

'Look, last night I thought I was being overcautious. Now I know I wasn't. These people have serious resources and you're right, they're trying to kill her.'

'Why?'

'I don't know. So Chris, you don't have to be my friend, but I need you to be cool. Ella needs you to be cool.' Chris nodded and Lucas handed him the key to the other room. 'Change in there, freshen up. Knock when you come back.'

Chris took the key but before opening the door he said, 'I'm sorry about the phone call.'

'It's my fault; I didn't make things clear. And this isn't the kind of work I usually do.'

'I don't understand. What do you usually do?'

'I kill people.' Chris stared at him as if to make sure he wasn't joking. He left then and Lucas locked the door and fell back into the armchair.

He knew one thing: killing people was easier than dealing with them, relating to them. And looking back over the last twenty-four hours, he'd done almost everything wrong. He hadn't spoken to them properly from the start and he hadn't made clear to them how serious things were and he'd overreacted with Chris when the person he was really angry with was himself.

He couldn't believe he'd been so sloppy, that he'd nearly let her get killed. Probably the only things that had saved her were her attractiveness and that innocently puzzled expression, and the fact that the gunman was young and stupid enough to be distracted by things like that.

But for all Lucas's shortcomings, she *was* still alive. And if he could get her out of Italy, he was confident enough she'd stay that way. What happened afterwards wasn't his concern.

The door opened and she came out of the bathroom, brushing her damp hair. She was wearing a tight-fitting top, a long hippyish skirt. It made her look taller than she was and highlighted her breasts, her hip bones, reminding him of the previous night, of thoughts he wanted to put out of his head, because they weren't appropriate, because there were more important things to think about.

'You look nice.' She responded with a token smile but looked immediately concerned as she glanced around the room and saw no Chris. 'He's getting changed in my room.'

'How is he?'

'Okay.'

She looked down at the floor for a second, then looked him in the face again and said, 'It was unforgivable, what you did.'

His thoughts foundered. Albeit in a shambolic fashion, he'd saved her life twice in the last twenty-four hours and killed three people in the process. But it was unforgivable that he'd made her boyfriend piss his pants for nearly getting her killed.

Even so, he could see how it had to look from her point of view. She'd been enjoying a tour of Europe with a guy she was in love with and this nightmare had descended over them, a nightmare of which the only physical embodiment was Lucas himself.

She was scared, worried, probably with good reason, and she had nobody else to offload any of it onto.

'You're right, it was unforgivable.' He thought of adding something else but didn't think he could stretch himself convincingly to contrition. 'Put the other things you bought into one of the new bags. We need to leave soon.' She looked like she wanted to say something else too, but after a pause she set to work packing the bag.

There was a knock at the door and Chris said, 'It's Craig.'

Lucas let him in and repeated the instructions he'd given to Ella, sparing him the awkward silence. When they were ready, he said, 'Okay, Chris, when you spoke to your brother last night, did you say anything about me?'

Chris shook his head vigorously and said, 'I didn't even tell him anything was wrong, just that we'd come back to Florence and that we were staying here. That's all, I just wanted them to know . . .' His words trailed off, probably with the raw memory of their last exchange on this subject.

'That's good.' He faced both of them again and said, 'Between here and the railway station I need you to be relaxed but stay tight, vigilant, and do everything I say. If I go down, you do anything—throw your bags at them, use a gun if you can reach one, and run, get to the police. Okay?' They nodded uneasily, perhaps at the thought of him being taken down, having to do this alone. 'Good. Let's go.'

Chris had the new backpack but Lucas gave him his other bag too. Ella had the duffel bag and Lucas his own backpack. He led them out into the corridor and through the reception, where there was still no one behind the desk. They could hear the sound of a TV from an adjoining room.

He hesitated by the elevator. It was an old-fashioned cage, making them too easy a target for anyone waiting at the bottom. He pointed at the stairs and put his finger to his lips. They walked quietly behind him, their steps lost against the steadily growing noise of the street below.

He stopped them a half-flight short of the bottom and went down to check out the lobby. There was only one person down there and it wouldn't be long before he was attracting flies. Lucas walked to the open street door, searched out a taxi and waved it over, at the same time checking the street, a cafe along the way in particular.

He went back into the lobby and waved them down. By the time they reached the street door the taxi driver was standing there, the trunk open, ready for the luggage.

'Santa Maria Novella,' said Lucas, and then retreated into the lobby. 'Chris, you put the bags in the car.' Chris carried the bags out on his own and the driver looked on, nonplussed, glancing in a couple of times to where Lucas stood with Ella in the shadows. 'You get in the front, Chris. Ella, you sit behind the driver.' As they stepped out into the barrier of heat, Lucas scanned the street again, taking in the cafe, cars, doorways, people walking. There was nothing he could see. Once he was sitting in the taxi, he pulled his gun, holding it casually by the side of his leg. He kept scanning the people and the traffic around them, stepping up a gear every time they slowed or stopped. The taxi driver could sense it, looking at Lucas in the rear-view a couple of times but turning away quickly whenever they made eye contact.

They hadn't been followed and, though any other time it would have been a classic danger point, he began to relax when they reached the railway station. He still moved them quickly, though, and drew the blinds as soon as they were inside their private compartment.

When the train started to move, Lucas released the blind on the window. The sunlight burst in, the air dancing with illuminated dust. Ella screwed her eyes up against the brightness, then looked at Lucas. 'Are we safe now?'

'I think so. No complacency, but you can take it easy for a while.' It was like he'd given them a muscle relaxant: both of them sank into their seats with relief.

'And you'll call my dad from Milan?'

'That's right. Three hours.' He caught a look from Chris and wondered if he suspected what that call might reveal. Possibly he thought Lucas already knew there was no one to call, that her father was dead. Lucas didn't know that for sure, but he was almost certain that's how it was, that somewhere along the line Hatto had upset someone enough for them to bring it back on his whole family. And it made him wish he *could* speak to Hatto now because he wanted to know what line he'd crossed, and on whose territory, to inspire a vengeance like this.

Twenty minutes out of Florence, Chris fell asleep. Ella was looking out the window and had been since they'd left. He wondered what she was thinking about, guessed it was probably just the whole storm of the last day, trying to make sense of it.

Not long after Chris had fallen asleep, she turned and stared at Lucas for a while, finally saying, 'I've been thinking about that man at the hotel.' He nodded, just to show that he was listening.

'You think he was there to kill me?' He nodded again, this time a regretful confirmation. She'd already reached that stage, though, of brushing to one side the fact that people were trying to kill her; she was deeper in than that. 'You see, that's what I don't understand, because he could've killed me, but he didn't. The way he was looking at me, it was like he'd changed his mind.'

'He might have changed it back,' said Lucas, attempting to dispel any doubt as to whether he'd needed to kill him or not. 'You're an attractive girl—it threw him. If someone more professional had been waiting in that lobby this morning, I would have lost you.'

She looked surprised by his words, misinterpreting them, perhaps, because she said, 'Would it have mattered to you, if you'd lost me?'

'To my pride, maybe my reputation. I don't know you well enough to care beyond that.'

'Is there anyone you do care about?'

The speed of her response threw him, a hemorrhage of faces and names, memories, all of them evaporating away into nothing in the hostile environment of his consciousness.

'Not anymore, not for a long time. I care about my books, my solitude.'

'You sound like an old man.' He smiled but didn't reply and she said, 'Have you got anything to read?'

'Sure. I've got *A Journal of the Plague Year* by Defoe—that's what I was going to read next, but you're welcome to have it. And you know I've got *The Nibelungenlied*. You should give it a try; it's a good story.'

She looked unconvinced but laughed a little and said, 'Go on then, I'll try it.' He was pleased. It wasn't often he got the chance to recommend books to people, let alone have them follow those recommendations. She might even finish it before they parted and want to discuss it with him.

The two of them sat opposite each other reading and Chris slept. It was like they were ordinary people on a straightforward journey. Maybe she still saw herself like that, unaware how deep this fault line ran. There might be a way back to an ordinary life for Chris but hers was changed for good.

Lucas found it appropriate somehow to be reading of rumors and the approach of plague, the steadily increasing tally of deaths. He'd become adept at shutting the present out while he was reading, but he was clicking off the minutes in the back of his head, conscious that this slumberous calm would be torn too soon.

About half an hour before they reached Milan, he stopped reading altogether, keeping his eyes on the book only to avoid conversation. Chris had woken and was checking his watch every few minutes. Ella was still reading but she was beginning to look restless too.

Lucas was calmer than they were but he was uncomfortable all the same, knowing that he could put it off no longer, make no more excuses. It almost made him wish they'd be ambushed again in the station, just for the further diversion it would cause.

It would have been a good place for them to take a pop at her too, but he was confident now that they were clear of trouble. Even so, he still played it cautious as he moved them to the next train, stung by the slip he'd made that morning.

Before leaving them in the new compartment, he gave Chris the gun again but told him to take it out only if he was certain they were in trouble, stressing that he thought they were over the worst. Then he left them, checked his watch and found a phone that was away from the telltale background noise of the station.

At first he thought it would run onto the answering machine again, but on maybe the last possible ring it was picked up and a woman said hello. He knew.

'I'm sorry, I must have the wrong number; I was trying to reach Mark Hatto.'

There was an awkward pause before the woman said, 'No, you have the right number. I'm a police officer. Could I ask who you are, sir?'

'Of course. I'm Philip Hatto, Mark's cousin. Now if you don't mind me asking, why are you there? Is everything okay?'

Another awkward pause, suggesting she was new to this aspect of her job.

'Do you have someone else there with you, Mr. Hatto?'

'My wife's here, but what's that got to do with anything? What's going on?' It was like he'd said to Chris that morning about watching movies: he knew the part he was playing, the script he was meant to use. It was probably the same script she'd used in role-play during her training.

'I'm afraid I have some very bad news, Mr. Hatto. We were called to the house this morning by a member of staff. I'm sorry to have to tell you that your cousin, his wife and son have all suffered gunshot wounds, each of them fatal.'

'They're dead?' He wanted to make sure she hadn't misused the word 'fatal' in her attempt to break the news gently.

'I'm afraid so.' He hung up the phone. It was what he'd expected, but it didn't mean anything to him. The news had all the impact of an election result in some country he'd never heard of.

The only thing that mattered to him was that he had to go back and tell Ella that her family had been killed, and he didn't know whether she was safe, whether she'd ever be safe. That was some news to break to a girl who'd been as close to death as she had been today.

As he walked back along the platform, a couple of pigeons took flight from his path and he followed their ascent for a few seconds, up into the vaulted sky of the terminus. For a moment, it seemed like he could still hear the flapping of their wings, even above the train noise and the background bustle of the station, and it gave him a strange sense of peace.

It made him want to be home and done with this. He was heading home, but the fragmented longing he'd just experienced had been for something more distant, unreachable: the touch and smell of skin, warmth, a laugh, a breeze off the sea . . . memories too painful to dwell upon, a sense of home that had never really belonged to him.

He knocked on the compartment door and waited for Chris to open it.

'I'll stay out here in the corridor until we leave the station. Close the door again.'

Chris nodded but from behind him Lucas heard Ella say, 'Did you speak to him?'

He looked over Chris's shoulder. He thought she'd come close to guessing a couple of times, but there it was in her face; for all her intelligence, for all that had happened, she didn't have a clue.

'No, I didn't. I'll explain once we're on the move.' She looked baffled but Lucas nodded for Chris to close the door. He had to wait, because she'd react badly and he needed the noise of the train's movement to drown out any sound of distress.

A couple of people squeezed past him in the narrow corridor and then the train started to ease along the platform, imperceptibly at first, the movement so smooth it looked like the neighboring train was moving. He waited till they were clear of the station, speed and racket building.

Maybe Chris had said something or maybe, given a few minutes to think about it, she'd begun to stack things up. Either way, as soon as he stepped inside she said, 'What's happened? Just tell me.'

'Your family's dead. The police answered the phone.' She didn't call out, didn't cry. It was like he'd spoken in a language she hardly knew and she was still translating in her head. Yet the expression on her face was familiar to him; it was how people looked after being shot.

Lucas heard Chris whispering, 'Shit, shit, shit,' and turned for a moment to look at him. He was sitting on the edge of the seat with his face buried in his cupped hands.

'All of them?'

He looked back at Ella and said, 'Yes, all shot, probably the same time as they tried to get you last night.'

'But why?'

'Your dad must've fucked someone off in a big way. And he had enemies.'

Her face and thoughts finally fused, dissolving into each other, a sudden violent retching of tears and emotion and strangled words.

'Ben didn't have enemies.' She could say no more, falling apart into sobs, and then Chris was holding her and she was clinging on to him. He was whispering words of comfort now and the more he said the tighter she held him.

Lucas stepped back outside and closed the door. At first he couldn't hear anything from inside the compartment, the train noise covering for them as he'd hoped. As his ears adjusted, though, her distraught cries became clearly audible and he started to look around uneasily, feeling exposed.

Someone came walking along the corridor, an elderly woman, too fat to pass him. The most natural thing would have been for him to give way by stepping back into his compartment, but he didn't want to open the door and let the distress contained there spill out.

Instead, he walked along a little way and ducked into an empty compartment to avoid making eye contact with the woman. He walked back then, and for the second time his ears tricked him into thinking she'd quietened. But it was still there, an incoherent wailing, growing louder, more intense.

And there was nothing he could do to help. He could keep Ella Hatto alive, he could kill for her, but he could offer no comfort, no compassion. He didn't have those things within him, and it made his skin crawl to stand there in earshot of her distress because it exposed him for who he was. He was a man with a gun, nothing more, and he didn't even want to be that.

Chapter Five

She puzzled over the skirt through the first fuzzy moments of wakefulness. She seemed to be wearing a long skirt, one she didn't recognize. She was slouched awkwardly and she felt if she moved she'd be able to see it properly and she'd understand.

Chris was holding her, though, and the train was rocking gently and she didn't want to move. And then from the corner of her eye she saw someone else in the compartment with them, and then recognition: Lucas.

She jumped up in the seat, startled, full of dread. Chris released her. Lucas looked up from the book he was reading, curious perhaps, no more than that. She was about to say she'd had the most dreadful dream but her conscious thoughts had caught up with her.

Her family was dead. Lucas had told her. Men like those who'd tried to kill her had gone to their home and killed her parents, killed Ben. The tears started to form again, her throat tightening, but she fought clear of it, focusing on the moment.

'How do you feel?' She looked across at Lucas but the question hadn't been his. He was already reading again and she was puzzled as she looked at him, trying to work out if he was scared of her emotions, his own, anybody's, or if he just didn't feel anything at all.

There had been moments in the last twenty-four hours when she'd thought there had to be something more to him, softer depths. That morning with Chris, the conversation she'd overheard from the bathroom, and just the way he was seeing them through this—it all gave the impression that they were more than just a job to him.

But looking at him now she had her doubts. He wasn't like they were. It didn't matter anyway; Lucas didn't matter—not against being alone, not against half of who she was being erased like that.

And she still couldn't find a way to register that fact. It was too big, too final. How could they be gone? How could Ben not be there? It seemed so unreal that she began to speculate on the ways in which Lucas could have been mistaken. Or possibly he was lying—like Chris had said, they didn't really know who he was or that her dad had sent him.

'Ella? How do you feel?' Chris's face and that question and she knew it was true. They were dead. She'd cried herself to exhaustion, her jaw aching still, and yet even now she felt like she didn't have the space, the distance, the facts, any of the things she needed to come to terms with it.

'I don't know,' she said, finally answering him, and her own voice sounded strange, like she was underwater, or lost in some heart-sickening dream.

'I went and got some drinks. Do you want some? Coke? Water?'

'Water, please.' He handed her the bottle. The water was warm but she took a couple of mouthfuls, then more as she realized how dry her throat was.

At first she thought it was getting dark but looking out of the window, she saw the sky was overcast and that the landscape they were passing through was alpine and damp.

'Are we in Switzerland?'

Lucas looked away from his book long enough to check his watch but didn't answer.

'You've been asleep for a few hours,' said Chris.

'If you want to freshen up you should do it now. We'll be there soon and then it's about a thirty-minute drive.'

'Where are we going?' She had nowhere to go, nothing to return to, a truth that should have torn her again but all her pain was dulled now, smothered by the emotional fatigue that was in every cell, every nerve ending. She felt like nothing would ever shock or hurt her again.

'I'm taking you to my place for a night or two. Then I'll take you into Zurich and hand you over to the consulate.'

She looked at Chris and realized they'd discussed it while she'd been sleeping. It bothered her, though she wasn't sure why.

'What will the consulate do with me?'

'I imagine they'll repatriate you.'

'I mean, where will I go?'

Lucas looked baffled for a second before saying, 'You're an adult. You can go wherever you want.' It made her feel spoiled and pathetic to think of herself as someone helpless while he saw her as an adult, someone capable of looking after herself. He seemed to reconsider, though, and added, 'I suppose they might suggest you go to your uncle or any other family you've got.'

She didn't have any other family and now she imagined the scenario getting worse, knowing that Simon was a partner in the business, that he was as likely to be a target of the killers as her father had been.

'What if they killed my uncle, too?'

He thought about it for a while, apparently weighing things up.

'It's possible, but your dad's the one who was connected.'

'Connected? Your dad was like a gangster?'

She looked at Chris, trying to work out from his expression whether he was impressed or disgusted by the possibility. It was what Lucas seemed to be suggesting, but her dad was anything but gangster material. He'd always been a benign presence in the house, distant but loving.

She looked questioningly at Lucas but he glanced in turn at Chris, as if to ask whether it was wise to discuss this kind of family business in front of him. It was laughable, given what he'd seen, given too that it was business she hadn't known about herself until now.

'I've got no secrets from Chris.'

Lucas shrugged and said, 'He was no gangster. He knew a few but he was never in organized crime himself. He started dealing drugs in the late sixties, made a lot of money, invested in property, moved into the arms trade. Then the drugs led him into financial services, offshore banking, that kind of thing, cleaning other people's drug profits. And he kept investing, buying up property, legitimate financial concerns, IT companies, you name it. He was a good guy.'

She stared at him in disbelief. Only the final five words had reminded her of the man she'd known as her father and she couldn't quite work out how Lucas had slipped them in, how they'd seemed to him like a fitting conclusion to all the sleaziness he'd just described.

It couldn't be right anyway. How could her family have had secrets like that at its core without her ever knowing or even sus-pecting? Surely her mother had known, and yet there'd never been any sense of disquiet or concern, never any attention from the police, never any fears about security.

Lucas had to be wrong or it was like her whole life had been a lie, her parents recast as strangers, her memories false. Only Ben remained true because he'd been kept as ignorant as she had, and now he was dead and would never have the slightest idea why.

She started to imagine how it might have been, whether the killers had gathered them all together first, or killed them wherever they'd found them in the house, whether Ben had had time to be scared. She backed off, though, the thoughts too precipitous.

It took an effort to block it out again but then she said, 'You're mistaken. If my dad told you all that stuff, he was probably just trying to impress you or something.'

'What makes you think that would impress me?' Lucas looked momentarily offended but appeared to soften again and said, 'He filled in the details and the backstory. The rest was out there— he was a player.' She put together what he was saying with all that had happened but as if reading her mind, he said, 'Don't jump to conclusions. To me, this smacks of payback from long ago. You know, in a business where people disappear for fifteen-, twenty-year stretches, you can never completely forget about the enemies you made in the past. Someone who orchestrates the death of an entire family strikes me as someone who's had a long time to think about things.'

She looked at Chris, wanting an expression from him of sharing her incredulity. She couldn't quite meet his eyes, though; there was a look on his face like his thoughts were tumbling as fast as hers but in a different direction. She wanted at least some communication with someone who'd make her feel less alone in this, but all she had was Lucas, redrawing the map of her world.

'I'm sure you'll understand that it's quite difficult for me to take all this on board.'

'What's to take on board? Your dad was okay. He had a good run in a risky business. Now he's dead.' Then he added, like an afterthought, 'And of course, you're now a very wealthy young woman.'

She laughed in shock, wanting to distance herself from everything he'd been saying, wanting Chris to see that she was distancing herself from it.

'I don't want that kind of money.'

'Trust me, there's only one kind of money. And if you think otherwise, if you think the interest on your savings is clean, then you really do have a lot to take on board.'

'That's ridiculous,' said Chris, suddenly animated. 'You're honestly trying to suggest there are no ethical ways of making money?'

Lucas said only, 'We're here. Get your bags together.' He stood up and she noticed the train was slowing.

They had to be safe here, wherever they were, but even now Lucas hurried them through the station. She searched for a name board but couldn't see one and a moment later they were standing next to a sleek black Mercedes.

He opened the trunk for the bags and Ella said, 'Do you mind if I sit in the front this time?'

'Feel free.'

They got in and drove off, climbing steadily away from the town. It was just before six by the clock on the dash, still too early for sunset, but the cloud cover had sewn dusk into the fabric, and after a few minutes of driving, a fine drizzle added to the sense that they were losing themselves in a dark landscape.

Lucas pointed and said, 'There are CDs in there. Why don't you choose something to put on?' She opened the glove compartment and took the CD off the top.

'I love Nick Drake,' she said. 'My dad has the original record of this.'

'I've only been into him for a couple of years.'

'Did my dad recommend him? He's always banging on about music from the sixties.' She wondered if that was how he'd come to deal drugs, not as a criminal but as a youthful idealist.

Lucas smiled and said, 'Your dad and me, we were never . . . Well, we never discussed music. Amazon recommended it to me.' Ella smiled too, amused somehow because nearly every song she loved was associated with a moment, a person, an event, and yet here was Lucas, taking his cues from an algorithm.

She put the CD in the player and relaxed into her seat as the soft lull of the music started, the windshield wipers gliding silently in front of her. She felt warm and secure, the car moving smoothly through the sodden landscape, the rain hanging in the air like mist. It was like they were driving through the ragged edges of clouds.

'Sorry about your family.' She looked at him, surprised, touched too, even though it was little more than a politeness, one that might have come several hours earlier at that. But after one day of knowing him, she sensed it was probably a departure for Lucas to be expressing sorrow or regret for anything.

'Thanks. I appreciate it.' She thought suddenly of that morning, of Lucas gently wiping the blood from her face, his fingers sensitive, caring. She'd been too shocked to take it in at the time but the memory of it now made her realize there was something she should have said earlier too, an omission that was understandable, perhaps, in her case but that still needed to be put right. 'And, Lucas. Thank you.' He glanced across at her, uncertain. 'For saving my life.'

'It's what I was sent to do.'

That was it, the door was closed again, but she hadn't been mistaken; that other person was there, somewhere. She said no more either, but sat and listened to the music and watched the world sliding by and tried to keep her mind hitched up there on the immediate, on the passing moments. She was too spent to let it go anywhere else.

The time would come soon enough anyway, when she'd have to think about those things again. And she'd be forced to face the facts of how they'd died, of who they'd been, of the uncertain future that lay ahead of her.

That was all out there, and maybe it was selfish, but for a few hours she wanted to pretend like it hadn't happened. 'River Man' was playing, a song she wanted to associate in her memory with this drive, with Lucas and Chris, but with nothing else.

They passed through a small village, then through a mix of pasture and dense woods. She counted only two other houses, warmly lit, and then ten minutes after leaving the village they turned onto a narrower track, following it for a few hundred yards until they reached his place.

When she got out of the car, she could understand the appeal; the rain had stopped and the air felt intimately close, the silence like held breath. The house was layered in shadows. It looked like a traditional alpine house—the outline, the balcony stretching across the front. It was modern, though, timber and glass.

'Did you build this?'

He was at the trunk, getting the bags out.

'No, the guy who built it died, and his wife didn't want to stay here afterwards. Lucky for me.' They made towards the house, but after a few steps he turned to say, 'He died of cancer.'

They followed him up the stairs into a small porch where he stopped to turn on the lights and check what looked like a complex alarm system. He led them into a large room then: living room, dining room, kitchen, spread across the whole upper story, the walls lined with books.

'I'm not really geared up for visitors but make yourselves at home.' He gestured towards an internal staircase. 'Guest bedroom and bathroom are downstairs at the back.'

Ella looked at Chris with a smile and held her bag out.

'Sure, I'll take the bags down.' He turned to Lucas and said, 'Want me to take yours?'

Lucas seemed amused by the offer but said, 'Thanks. Mine's the bedroom at the front.'

Ella walked around the room, which looked amazingly tidy. She noticed some unopened letters on a side table, so she guessed he had someone come in while he was away. She altered her course slightly so that she could pass close enough to see what was written on them.

It took her by surprise, not because it wasn't his name, but because they were all addressed to 'S. Lucas.' She turned to find him looking at her from across the room.

'Lucas is your surname,' she said, brushing off the embarrassment of being caught snooping.

'Yes.'

'What does the S stand for?'

'Stephen.'

'Amazing. I don't know why but I assumed Lucas was your first name.' She thought about it for a second and said, 'Can I call you Stephen?'

'I've always been Lucas. One person years ago insisted on Luke. Never Stephen.'

'What about your parents? Surely they called you Stephen?'

'It's always been Lucas.' She wasn't sure what he meant by that, but it was clearly something that wasn't up for discussion.

'You have a lot of books,' she said, looking for an obvious way out.

'You should see the bedrooms.' It was Chris, emerging from the stairs.

Lucas laughed and said, 'It's my passion. Not special editions or anything, just books. I love to read.'

'This is a great house,' said Chris.

'I like it.' He looked around, uncertain, possibly even uncomfortable. 'Like I said, make yourselves at home. I'll cook some pasta or something. Tomorrow I'll make some phone calls, see how the dust has settled. Hopefully the next day I'll take you into

Zurich.' He nodded as if to himself and walked away into the kitchen area.

Ella looked again at the unopened mail, wondering when he'd bother to look through it, when he'd check his answering machine. He gave the impression of someone who lived like a ghost, the demands of everyday life no longer registering with him.

Chris walked out onto the balcony and she followed him, looking at the view that was slowly closing down in front of them: woods turning into solid blocks of shadow, swaths of pasture floating hazily. On a clear day there were probably distant mountains but this evening the sky had fallen, smothering everything.

They stood at first without saying anything, but then Chris said, 'I'm sorry if I haven't been much good the last day and a half. It's just been like one shock after another but I should have stopped to think, how it's been . . .' The last word caught in his throat. She turned to look at him and he smiled, clearing his throat before saying, 'I'm just saying sorry for being a prick.'

She shook her head and held him, drawing in tighter against him as he put his arms around her. She felt like this was all she needed, all the security she needed—to stand here enfolded in his arms, his breath hot on her neck, hands gently rubbing her back.

She listened to the sound of the water dropping from the eaves and the trees, a dog's bark carrying from a long way off, and behind them, equally faint, the comforting domestic sound of food being prepared. That was where her thoughts ran aground, because the man preparing that food was Lucas, and the sense of respite she felt here was false.

Lucas simply continued to read his book as he ate his dinner. Ella and Chris sat opposite each other further down the table, silent, and they waited till Lucas had finished before complimenting him on the meal. He thanked them and refused the offer of help with the dishes.

When he came back to them, he said, 'Do you play chess, or backgammon?'

'I play chess,' said Chris. 'We both play backgammon.'

Lucas nodded, went to a cupboard and took out a large leather backgammon board, opening it on a coffee table between the two sofas. 'Help yourselves to drinks,' he said and took his book to a chair on the other side of the room, close to the windows that opened out onto the balcony.

They played backgammon, almost totally ignored by Lucas. Ella couldn't concentrate, the game not offering enough of a diversion from the thoughts waiting to grind back over her. Distant thunder sounded on and off throughout the evening and occasionally a heavier roll would cause them to stare out beyond the windows.

The storm was still hovering when Ella woke in the early hours. She'd been startled awake by a lurch in her dreams, a heaving sequence of violent flashbacks, her jaw tight when she woke, heart fighting.

She looked up at the felt blackness of the room, listened to Chris breathing next to her, remembered where she was. It was the second time she'd woken since hearing the news and already it came as less of a shock to remember what had happened, more a leaden realization that this was the truth now, that her old life had been a dream.

Hidden away there in the night, she allowed herself to think about it, picturing their faces, trying to take in that they were no longer simply far away but gone. But as soon as she thought of Ben, the tears started to gather in her eyes and she felt like she'd collapse in on herself.

Why was it Ben more than her mum and dad? She'd loved them all equally but it was his loss she felt, perhaps because it was the one she'd never once contemplated, and because he hadn't even lived—college, traveling on his own. He'd never even had a real girlfriend.

She jumped up from the bed, eager to escape the snare of thoughts that lay in wait there. She found her way into the bathroom and washed her face, then jumped as a roll of thunder cracked overhead, the wooden frame of the house vibrating with it.

She turned to walk back out and smiled as she noticed two neat white bathrobes hanging on the back of the door, like in a hotel. It made her wish she was majoring in psychology, to know what it meant for a man who wasn't used to visitors to put this much effort into his guest room.

Putting one of the robes on, she stopped to listen for Chris's slow, rhythmic breathing before continuing out of the bedroom and up to the living room. A small lamp was on up there and as she reached the top of the stairs, she could see Lucas standing out on the balcony.

Ella saw him turn to check who'd come up before switching his attention back to the storm. She walked over to him and said, 'I'm not disturbing you, am I?'

'No.' She automatically expected him to ask a typical small-talk question, like why couldn't she sleep; it was still catching her out, the lack of conversational glue in his speech. For a second, they were both illuminated like they'd been hit by a strobe in a nightclub. The thunder exploded overhead, the long aftershock of a plane going through the sound barrier.

When the noise had died down, Lucas said, 'It was during a storm that Mary Shelley started *Frankenstein*. Lake Geneva. The same evening, Polidori started work on one of the precursors to *Dracula*.'

'Yeah, I knew that. It was Byron's idea. Some people think Byron wrote the Polidori book.'

'Oh.' He turned, captured, it seemed, by a piece of information he hadn't heard before. 'I haven't read *The Vampyre*. Didn't like *Dracula* much. I loved *Frankenstein*.'

'Really? I found it hard work.'

He didn't respond at first but then, as if remembering his responsibilities as a host, he said, 'Would you like a glass of milk or something?'

'What's that you're drinking?'

'Cognac. Want some?'

'Please.' He went back inside and she walked in and sat within the pool of light that came off the small lamp.

There was a photograph in a simple frame next to the lamp, inconspicuous, but she noticed it now because the rest of the room was dark. It was a girl of about her own age, maybe a little older, very pretty, long fair hair. It had been taken on a beach or at least near the sea, the girl's smile carefree, like she'd been caught in the middle of a laugh.

It was the only thing she'd seen in the whole house that was suggestive of him having contact with another human being, attachments, people who mattered to him. When he came over with the drink, she thanked him and said, 'Is that your daughter?'

He looked at the picture and said, 'How old do you think I am?' She wasn't sure. He didn't look that old but he'd talked about her father and she'd started to imagine them being the same age, which they obviously weren't.

'How old are you?'

'I'm forty-two, and she's an old girlfriend. Someone I knew a long time ago. I don't even know why I keep it.'

She looked at the picture and back at him, daring to tease him a little.

'Perhaps because she still means something to you?'

'Maybe. Maybe you don't know me well enough to analyze me.'

She shrugged it off and sipped at the cognac, fiercer in the mouth than she'd expected. 'What's her name?'

'Madeleine,' he said, sitting down.

'That's a nice name.'

'Yes, I think of Proust every time I look at her.' She could tell he'd made some kind of joke but she didn't get it and couldn't see how it was meant to be funny.

'Sorry?'

'Nothing.' He looked apologetic, maybe acknowledging that it hadn't been that funny. 'She was French, and that picture was taken a long time ago. I haven't seen her in fourteen years or more.'

'Wow.' She wasn't surprised, but it seemed like an appropriate response. 'You're single now?'

He laughed as he said, 'Yes.'

'Do you have any kids at all?'

'You ask a lot of questions.' There he was, backing off again, but she felt confident enough to pursue him.

'It's what people do when they're getting to know each other.'

'Why would you want to get to know me?'

The question was close to being hostile but she said, 'Why not? You're worth knowing, aren't you? You're smart, you read, you kill bad guys.'

He smiled, but to himself this time, and looked lost in thought. The room crackled with light again, the thunder following after a few seconds.

'It's moving away.'

She turned briefly towards the window as if there were something to see, but came back to him, saying, 'So? Do you have kids?'

He looked mildly exasperated. 'I can't see why it's so important to you but yes, I have a daughter, with Madeleine. I've never seen her.'

'How sad. You haven't had any contact at all?'

'Nothing. She didn't even want my money. She was wealthy anyway, but I think she'd have lived in the gutter rather than take it. She made me promise to disappear, never get in touch.'

'But why?'

'You don't get it, do you? See, I *am* the bad guy. Madeleine didn't get it either, not until too late. I'm not someone who's good to be around, especially a child.'

She didn't want to know about this. Until now she'd pictured him as a bodyguard, working in the underworld maybe, but not a criminal himself. The kind of person who averted misery, not inflicted it. Surely her dad wouldn't have employed him otherwise, and her dad knew him.

'Tell me how you met my father.'

His spirits appeared to pick up.

'Windhoek. 1982. Windhoek—it's in Namibia. I had a lot of attitude back then, arrogant, but Hatto was a cool guy. He asked me to do some work for him. That was it. We never became friends or anything; we just hit it off. I trusted him.'

She was still trying to take in the description of her father as a 'cool guy,' a sentiment she'd heard a couple of times before from Simon, from her mother, people whose opinions hadn't carried much weight. Ben was pretty cool, though, so maybe he'd been cool like Ben.

There was another flash of lightning, the room theatrically lit for a moment before the dark closed in again around the lamp and the two of them sitting there. She counted to four before the thunder sounded, and felt a little sad, the way she always did when a storm retreated.

She sipped at her cognac, growing accustomed to it, and then as the thought occurred to her she said, 'I should make a will.'

He nodded, saying, 'I suppose so, when you get back home.'

'Don't you know anyone here? What if my plane crashes? What if someone else tries to kill me?' It was something she'd never thought about before, making a will, but suddenly it felt urgent, even though there was no one to leave anything to except her uncle or her two young cousins. She didn't even know what she'd be leaving; only the hazy phantom fortune Lucas had suggested.

'It's Sunday tomorrow. But I might be able to arrange something, just to put your mind at rest till you get back.'

'Good.' She finished her drink and nestled further into the sofa. 'You should write to your daughter.'

'How can I? I don't even know her name.'

⌣

When Ella woke, she was still on the sofa, a blanket over her. It was light, a clear blue sky visible through the windows. She could hear sounds coming in from the kitchen, and she could smell coffee. She sat up, but it was Chris in the kitchen, not Lucas.

He saw her and lifted his hand. A minute later he came over carrying a tray with coffee on it, two cups. He looked fresh, like he'd slept right through the storm.

'Morning. How did you sleep?'

'Okay, I think. I came up here because the storm woke me.'

'I know. Lucas told me.'

'Oh, he's up?'

Chris raised his eyebrows and said, 'When I got up, he'd just come back from his run. He's already gone back out, said he won't be long.' He kissed her on the top of the head and sat down. She glanced across at the lamp, then did a double-take: the photograph was gone. She puzzled over why he might have moved it. Then Chris interrupted her thoughts, saying, 'It's beautiful here.

Lucas said we can go out walking this afternoon if we like, just the two of us.'

'I'm sure you'll both have a lovely time.'

Chris laughed. She almost laughed too but felt guilty, a guilt she knew was stupid but couldn't help, because she'd made a joke and her parents and brother were lying in a morgue somewhere.

A car sounded in the distance and they both looked towards the balcony. Ella walked over. She could still hear the car, the sound probably carrying from a long way off. It sounded like it was headed in their direction and for a moment she thought about what to do if it wasn't Lucas, if it was another gunman. He wouldn't have left them alone, though, not if he'd thought there was any danger out there. A few minutes later his car emerged down the lane, splashing through the puddles from the night's rain.

She went back in as he came through the door. He smiled and said, 'Your uncle and his family are safe. They're under police protection.'

'Did you speak to them?'

Lucas looked nonplussed by the suggestion and said simply, 'No.'

'Still,' she said, 'it's something to be thankful for.' Even so, a voice in her head was asking why it couldn't have been them instead of her parents and brother.

'Now, get dressed. If you still want to do it, a friend of mine has agreed to put you a will together.'

'Good.' Chris looked surprised, a quizzical expression which she responded to by kissing him and saying, 'Thanks for the coffee.'

She took a shower and came back up wearing more of the new clothes they'd bought in Florence. They were hers but she couldn't help feeling she'd borrowed them, as if everything she'd had in the world had been lost, as if she had to go back to the drawing board, left with nothing except Chris, and maybe not even him.

He stood up as she came into the room and said, 'Do you want me to come with you?' He didn't want to go, clearly, but wanted to make it her choice.

'Not if you don't want to. I'm probably gonna have to do a lot of things on my own in the next few days.' He nodded but looked relieved, and she was suddenly angry with him.

'Okay, Chris, you know the score.' Chris nodded sheepishly, because he'd already failed them on that count once before.

Ella and Lucas left in silence but as they drove away she said, 'I think he'll break up with me.'

'He might. You're both young, but you have to grow up fast and maybe he doesn't want to. Why should he?' His response threw her. It shouldn't have, but she'd half expected the reassurance she'd been fishing for. 'Were you waiting for me to tell you everything's going to be fine?'

'No,' she said, too insistent.

'Good, because it won't be. Life's cruel—anyone who thinks otherwise is living a lie.'

'You're wrong.' Possibly he was right about Chris but she wasn't ready to let go completely. She had to believe she'd find a way back to normality, to the kind of life she'd always imagined for her future. 'I mean, I can see why you think that way but most people lead perfectly happy lives, and even when there are tragedies, they carry on, they have friends, people they love.'

He kept his eyes on the road. He looked like he was thinking about an answer, but if he was it never materialized. It left her feeling like he'd won the point, exasperated, unable to decide whether his social skills were nonexistent or highly advanced and manipulative.

She let it drop and said, 'So where are we going?'

'To see Max Caflisch. He's a lawyer, and given the circumstances, he's agreed to meet us at his office.'

'You said he was a friend of yours.'

'Well, the word "acquaintance" is a little anal, don't you think?' He was making another of his bizarre little jokes, but this time she was smiling, then laughing. Lucas almost looked put out, as if he never really expected anyone to find him funny.

They drove into the small town. She guessed it was the same one they'd arrived in the previous day but she couldn't be sure. It looked traditional, like something operated by clockwork. For the most part, it was quiet and empty.

Lucas pulled up behind a parked car and as he came to a stop, two people got out, a man with dark hair and glasses and a girl of about Ella's age, obviously his daughter. The man moved quickly, opening Ella's door for her, and as she stepped out he said, 'Delighted to meet you, Ella, and sorry only that it couldn't be with better circumstances. I'm Max Caflisch.' She shook his hand. 'And my daughter, Katharina—she'll be a witness for us.'

'Hi.'

Ella shook her hand too and the girl said, 'I'm sorry to hear about your family.'

'Thank you. And thank you, Mr. Caflisch, for agreeing to see me.'

'Of course. Now, let's go into my office.' He took the key and opened the door, leading them upstairs into a small wood-paneled reception and through to his office.

Once they were sitting down he said, 'So, with my small understanding of your legal system, I believe a clearly worded and witnessed document is more than sufficient to be legal. But I must advise you, as soon as you return home, to attend to the issue there.'

'Of course.'

'Good. So, you know to whom you will leave your estate?'

'Yes, I want to leave everything to my uncle, Simon Hatto, and if he dies before me, for it to be divided equally between my cousins, George and Harry Hatto.'

He handed her a piece of paper and said, 'Please, write their full names and addresses, and yours also.' When she passed it back, he said, 'Fine. Now, you must excuse me.' He got up and left the room.

She turned in her chair, noticing for the first time that Katharina had pulled the other chair to a discreet distance and sat down. Lucas was standing near the door like he was on duty, his face betraying a total lack of interest in what was going on here.

'You are studying at college?' Katharina asked.

'Yes, English literature. And you?'

Katharina smiled, 'Law.' Ella felt acutely envious of this girl, following in the footsteps of her genial, provincial lawyer father.

Ella had never given much thought to what she wanted to do. She'd certainly never thought of following in her father's footsteps, not least because she'd never known the truth, had never sought it, always happy to settle for the humdrum catchall descriptions— financial services, something in the city.

And now, by default, that's who she'd become. She'd been handed a chalice that only someone like Lucas could consider untainted. She didn't want it, and didn't see why she couldn't leave it in Simon's hands or sell her way out and carry on with her life.

When Max came back in, it took only a few more minutes and they were done. She looked at Lucas and felt embarrassed, sensing now that maybe the whole business could have waited till she was back home.

As she made towards the door, she noticed a desk laid out with leaflets. In the middle of the selection was one with a rakish-looking puppy on it, staring out beseechingly. She stopped, and Max said, 'Yes, these are charities. Some people like to give money to charity. Of course, some people have no one else to give it to, so . . .' He pointed at the leaflet with the puppy on it and said, 'This is for the dogs, naturally.'

She smiled. The last two days had been a nightmare, like flying blind through a storm, and as things had deteriorated, it had felt like she was beyond ever taking control again.

If anything, worse was probably still to come, but something about being here with this benign man and his daughter, his collection of charity leaflets, made her feel like there was still some kind of life she could head for, some integral part of her family that they hadn't managed to destroy.

There were black days ahead, and a loss that would last forever, but she had to believe that, at some point in the distant future, all of this would turn back to the good. All she had to do was stay alive long enough to get there, a thought that made her want to hold on to Lucas, to take him back to England with her, because it was hard to imagine herself safe without him.

Part Two

Chapter Six

H e was free again, lesson learned. From now on, no matter who called, no matter what the history between them, he couldn't help them. This hadn't been too bad and they were nice enough kids, but the fact remained, he was either retired or he wasn't.

He thought of them now as he walked back into the station, how thrown they'd looked when he'd put them in a taxi and sent them in the direction of the consulate. They'd obviously expected him to go along, not appreciating that it wouldn't have been in anyone's interests for him to have shown up with them.

They'd be okay without him now anyway. Since Ella had made the call early that morning the consular staff would have been busy phoning around, checking her story, making arrangements. They probably already had a flight home, and that had been the limit of his job, delivering her into that security.

He was glad she'd gone. As much as he'd liked her, having her around had made him think of things that weren't worth thinking about. Maybe that had started before Montecatini, just watching them, but it had been worse afterwards—talking to her, having her stay in his house, the questions she'd asked.

He was distracted now by a girl walking through the station concourse who'd changed direction suddenly and headed towards him. For a split second, he tightened up but then noticed the scrunched-up bag in her hand, the litter bin next to the bench he was sitting on. She threw the bag in and changed course again, probably not even noticing him.

He looked around at the other people—a little kid dancing around as he walked in front of his parents, an old woman making steady progress with a small wheeled case, a look of long-nurtured disdain on her face, a couple of teenagers laughing. He took a mental snapshot of each of them, amazed as ever that it was probably the closest he'd come to knowing these people.

It was the thing that got him about railway stations and traveling by train. He'd often think of the houses he passed, the lit windows, cars waiting at crossings, people walking. A procession of glimpses into lives he'd never know.

He'd always found it vaguely depressing, and yet it shouldn't have mattered that the world was full of people he'd never know when he'd removed himself so completely from the world anyway. This time, though, waiting for a train, he understood why he felt like that.

His daughter could be one of these people. She could brush past him one day in a railway station or an airport and he wouldn't know, neither of them would ever know, that the opportunity of two lifetimes had come and gone, lost in the quickly forgotten detail.

He took a deep breath and snapped himself out of it. All these things were true, almost certainly, but life was full of poignant truths and wrongs that could never be righted. There was nothing to be gained from wallowing in them.

He took out the book he'd just bought, *Persuasion*, losing himself immediately in the distant history of the Elliot family. His routine had been upset, that was all, unsettling him. He'd get over it in a day or two.

By the time he got home, he felt better but the house itself was full of reminders, associations it would probably take him a while to erase. That was the trouble with allowing people to encroach on his solitude like that: their presence had a way of lingering on, throwing his life into bleak relief.

As soon as he walked in, he was drawn to the gun on the dining table, the one he'd taken from the guy in the hotel lobby. In the rush and confusion of leaving the hotel, Ella had packed it and had found it again only as they'd readied themselves to leave for Zurich that morning.

She'd tried to give back his copy of *The Nibelungenlied* too, but he'd told her to keep it. He'd written his number inside the cover and told her to call if ever she needed his help. He was already regretting that act of largesse and hoped only that she'd never find the need. If she did, he'd have to make his excuses, maybe point her in Dan Borowski's direction.

Even so, he could understand why he'd made the offer. In some subtle way she'd managed to get under his skin, a fact that reminded him of his next move on his return to normality. He took the picture of Madeleine out of the drawer and placed it back where it belonged, the thought of that stupid Proust joke jarring momentarily. He didn't even like Proust.

He sat down, hooked by the picture, realizing how much he'd missed seeing it this last week or so. He was conscious of the absurdity of it, that he missed a photograph, but it was the only remnant in his life of a time and a woman that he missed more than he knew how to feel.

It was a link to something else too—the summer day captured there, the loving smile, a link to a part of him from which he'd been exiled, the growing world of his daughter. Ella had told him to contact her and he'd dismissed it, but he knew that that was what these last few years had really been about: his attempt to recast his life for her.

At first he'd fooled himself that it was all in case she tracked him down, that he wanted her to find a man other than the one Madeleine would have described to her. He knew now, though, particularly after what had happened to Ella in the last few days, that he didn't want to wait anymore, despite all the promises he'd made at the time. He wanted to see her. He wanted to see both of them.

The phone rang. He looked across the room at it, letting it ring a couple more times before picking it up.

'Lucas, it's Dan.'

'What have you got?' It didn't really matter anymore but he was curious all the same.

'Not much. Contrary to expectations, Mark Hatto didn't have any bloody enemies.'

'What about people who've been doing time?'

'Drew a blank there too. Believe me, mate, nobody wanted Mark Hatto dead.'

'Tell that to his daughter.'

'I mean nobody in the business. Couple of people suggested if we look closer to home we might find someone with a bit more to gain. Simon Hatto mean anything to you?' Lucas couldn't understand how he'd missed such an obvious suspect and yet the possibility had eluded him, another indication of how far removed from the game he'd become. Hatto's brother certainly had a lot to gain from killing the entire family. So maybe the motive hadn't been vengeance at all—at least not the all-consuming vengeance he'd imagined—but greed. 'So what do you think? Want me to look into it?'

'No,' said Lucas. 'Not for the time being anyway. It's out of my hands. But thanks.'

'No worries. Give me a call if you need anything.'

Lucas hung up the phone and walked over to the balcony. He stood there for a while with his eyes closed, breathing in the scent of the woods, picking out the birdsong, the vaguer sounds traveling up to him on still air. For a moment he felt like he'd open his eyes and see Ella and Chris walking back towards the house. They'd been nice kids, but he had to concentrate now on the things that mattered: a return to Paris, seeing his daughter, seeing Madeleine.

Maybe that wasn't even the right thing to do. For all he knew, Madeleine had married, had more kids, and they were happy, his daughter never giving him a thought. His reappearance in their lives could unbalance all of that, but it was a risk he had to take.

For the Hatto family, it was already finished, no time left to say the things they'd been meaning to say to each other, to make plans, to grow closer. They'd been a family and now they were down to one, just like he was, but at least he still had a way back.

His thoughts slipped back to what Dan had said, back to that memory of her and Chris walking out of the woods, of Ella curled up on the sofa. He didn't want to remember any of it, though, because he didn't want to think about the bloodied hands into which he might have delivered her.

He hoped Dan was wrong, that was all. If Simon Hatto had killed her family it had almost certainly been for the control of Hatto's empire, and if that was the case, he'd strike again as soon as the time was right. Dan had to be wrong or Ella was dead too—she just didn't know it.

Chapter Seven

Take as long as you want.'

She heard the door close gently behind her and she was left alone in the unpleasantly comfortable silence. For all the thick carpeting and subdued lighting, for all the easy-on-the-eye mediocrity of the furnishings, the truth remained defiant and uncompromising in the three caskets before her.

She moved closer, walking between her parents' caskets, and looked down at their faces. Their eyes were closed but the area around her dad's right eye looked messy somehow and heavily made up. His glasses were missing and she wasn't sure if this was standard practice or more evidence that he'd been shot through the eye.

Ella studied her mother's face, looking for the same telltale signs, but she found none and wondered where the fatal bullet might have struck. No doubt she'd find out in due course. No doubt she'd find out everything.

She realized what she was doing, looking at them as though they were exhibits, unable to connect them with the people she'd known. These were her parents and they were dead but she wasn't sure what she was meant to feel as she looked at them.

Walking back around the bottom of her mother's casket, she approached Ben's from the far side, her gaze still drawn over the top of it to their parents, putting the moment off as long as possible. She didn't know if she could stand to see him up close, but that was what she was there for.

At first it didn't look like Ben and in a fleeting second of hope she thought maybe there'd been some terrible mistake. It was him, though, his face simply lacking the fluidity and expression she'd known, a face she'd taken for granted and worn lightly in her memory because she'd thought it would always be there.

She tried to fix him in her mind, seeing him for the first time as a stranger would have done—that he was good-looking, that girls would have found him attractive. She was taking in the details – the shape of his mouth, his nose, eyebrows—and then she spotted the small white scar on the underside of his chin.

She'd done that, had pushed him off his bike when they'd been little, an act of spite, the result of which had so terrified her that she vowed never to hurt him again. She hadn't either, but seeing the scar now brought back the guilty memory: his small body splayed on the stone path, his desperate attempts not to cry.

A single sob convulsed through her body, violently clenching her chest cavity, her throat. She wouldn't be able to live with this; it was too great a burden to carry and she was too small, too weak. She covered her face with her hands, forcing herself to breathe through them, and when she recovered some of her composure she looked at him again.

She wanted to hold him, but was afraid to. She stroked his collar-length hair, silky smooth, careful to avoid touching the falsely healthy skin of his face. And finally she noticed what should have been obvious from the start: the small reconstructed patch on his forehead, just above his nose bone.

That's where he'd been shot, where his future, their future together as brother and sister, had been erased. It made her angry, an emotion stronger even than the sorrow, perhaps because she could at least direct it into a determination to see the killers caught and punished. It was the only thing she could do for them now.

She left, not looking back. When she stepped into the corridor, she didn't see anyone at first, but near the main door she found Simon waiting for her, sitting on a chair like a schoolboy in trouble.

He jumped up at the sight of her. She'd always thought of them as looking alike but now he looked much younger than her dad, his hair still brown, his face lean and fresh. And he was all at sea. She'd seen him reach for his phone three or four times before stopping and each time, she was certain, it was because the person he wanted to call was lying in there in a casket.

He smiled helplessly and said, 'Are you okay?' She nodded. 'Awkward business—probably best to get it out of the way.'

'Do they have any idea who might have done it?'

He grimaced slightly, saying, 'Not yet, and they'll want to speak to you about that.'

'They said they would, but why? What can I tell them?'

'I expect they'll just ask if Mark had any enemies that you know of, any arguments you might have overheard.' He looked around quickly and added, 'Might equally use this as an excuse to investigate the business—or at least, to get your permission to investigate. So if they ask to check records, accounts, anything like that, you just refer them to me.'

She felt uncomfortable, a sense that she was skipping any initiation and being fast-tracked straight into secrets she'd been shielded from her whole life.

'Simon, that's what I'd do anyway. I don't want to be part of the business; I'm too young. I have college to finish. I'm not ready.'

He smiled again, more warmly this time, and said, 'Don't worry, you won't have to. And I can't bring them back, but I promise you, I'll do everything in my power to get your life back as normal as possible.' He put his arm over her shoulder and led her gently towards the main doors. 'In the meantime, don't discuss any of this in front of the police. We'll talk in private back at the house.'

'Okay.'

One of the policemen was waiting outside and smiled sympathetically as he opened the door for them. He got in next to the driver and they started off for Simon's.

As they rode in silence, she got the feeling Simon was uncomfortable. Occasionally, the policeman in the passenger seat turned and offered up some friendly comment or sympathetic inquiry. Inappropriate as it was, Ella wanted to laugh at the effort he was making. She found herself thinking of Lucas and missing him, his abruptness and strange social tics.

She thought of Chris too, how two days ago in Switzerland, they'd made love in the woods, sex that had been passionate and desperate, perhaps because there'd been a sense of finality about it. She wanted to call him, see him, touch him.

'Do you mind if I call Chris later?'

Simon turned to her and said, 'Ella, you don't even need to ask. As long as you're staying with us, and that's as long as you like, you treat it as your home. We'll get your computer and everything, set it up in your room. We'll even get a separate phone line put in for you.'

She leaned over and kissed him on the cheek but then the police officer on the passenger side cleared his throat and said, 'Uh, I'm sure it's only a temporary measure, but I think we've taken the computers that were in the house for analysis.'

'You've taken my computer?'

'All of them. It's not that they've been seized or anything. It's just in case they contain anything that might help with the inquiry.'

Simon said, 'Inquiry into what?' He sounded angry. He took out his phone and punched in a number. 'Tim—Simon. The police have taken the computers from Mark's home, including Ella's, which has her college work on it and, I would imagine, strictly personal information. Get them back, would you? And fire a shot across their bows—remind them what they're investigating here: the murders of three innocent people.'

Ella was reeling. She couldn't understand why the police were being like this, helping her on the one hand and then treating her as someone who was a suspect. She'd seen it in the eyes of all the police personnel she'd met—a curiosity, wanting to know how much she knew.

Until last week she'd considered herself to be completely ordinary, a student from a comfortable middle-class family, respectable. Now their property was being impounded, the whole family being treated like they were in organized crime, a rumor that had even been leaked to the newspapers. Lucas had told her otherwise, though, and she had to hold on to that, at least until she could get to the truth herself.

The policemen at the house seemed more genuinely friendly, but then Lucy had been doing her classic country wife routine, giving them tea and cakes, and George and Harry had been harassing them. As they walked in, the boys went careering through the hall, shouting to Ella as they ran upstairs. Lucy came out to meet them and said, 'I thought I heard them call your name. How did it go?'

'Okay, I suppose. It's a strangely empty experience, isn't it? They're there and yet not there.'

'I know.'

'Luce, Ella and I need to talk business. I think as it's a beautiful day we'll sit out in the garden.'

'Of course,' she said, as if acknowledging a coded message. Then she added, 'I'll bring some drinks out. Is it too early for a gin fizz?'

'That'd be nice, actually,' Ella said. She found Lucy endearing like that; brought up in the city, she'd fallen in love with an idea of affluent country life that was about fifty years out of date.

This whole thing had probably shaken Lucy as much as it had any of them, forcing her to see how easily all of this could be taken away from her. She seemed to be holding up well enough now, but Ella could imagine how hard it would be once the police protection ended.

Simon led her across the large open lawn to the table and chairs under the oak tree. Ella wasted no time getting started. 'You need to tell me what kind of business we do. If I'm going to be speaking to the police and having my computer confiscated, I need to know the truth.'

'Of course.'

'No, wait. Two more things. First, before you give me a censored version, remember I'm entitled to find out for myself now. And second, I already know about the drugs and the arms trade, so don't spare me.'

Simon looked intrigued. 'How do you know about all of that?'

'The guy who protected me in Italy—he knew Dad a long time ago.'

'Did he now? Tell me more about this chap.'

She shook her head. 'First, you tell me about the business. Are we criminals?'

He laughed and said, 'Absolutely not. Look, Mark was involved in the drug business when he was young but that's ancient history. So is the arms business, but he never broke the law there anyway—some dubious export licenses here and there, but more often than not that was with the cooperation of the government.'

'So what about the police? And why did someone kill them?'

'That's two different questions. I'm assuming the contract is unfinished business from a long time ago.' The comment resonated with what Lucas had said, a corroboration that left her feeling queasy. 'The police business stems back mainly to the eighties. Mark was investigated by the US and UK authorities for money laundering. And I'll be honest with you, he *was* laundering back then, but they couldn't find anything. This is why your dad was successful: because he was good. Since the mid- to late eighties, the business has been legitimate anyway, but it's been kept complex and primarily offshore . . .' He stopped and looked across the lawn. Lucy was approaching, carrying a tray of drinks.

'Don't let me interrupt,' she said, the tone of a gentle admonishment.

'Nothing you don't know, Luce. Just the thought of a cold drink broke my train of thought.'

She smiled and said to Ella, 'I wouldn't be bringing him drinks if you weren't here.'

'Thanks,' said Ella, taking one of the condensation-frosted glasses.

As Lucy walked away, Simon said, 'As I was saying, the business has been kept complex and primarily offshore for the purposes of tax avoidance—not evasion, avoidance—so naturally, the authorities are still suspicious.'

'So you're saying I've got no reason to be ashamed or embarrassed.'

'Absolutely not. In fact you've every reason to be proud of what your dad achieved. Yes, there's an edge to the Hatto business empire, but we're not crooked, certainly not by wider corporate or government standards.'

She sipped at her drink, finding it less refreshing than she'd hoped, and said, 'Am I rich?'

'Yes. Very. Hard to put a precise figure on it but 80 per cent of the business—you're probably worth in excess of two hundred million.'

'That's impossible!' People with that much money didn't live like they had. 'I'm a multimillionaire?'

'Ella, please, your house alone makes you a multimillionaire.' The house. How could she ever go back there now?

'I want to sell the house as soon as possible.'

'Perhaps best not to rush into it. You might feel differently later in the summer.'

'No, I don't ever want to go back there. Will you arrange it, have everything put in storage, put the house on the market?' He nodded reluctantly. 'You don't mind me staying here the rest of the summer?'

'Of course not. And you'll join us in the Caribbean for Christmas.' She smiled, thinking, though, how she'd never have another Christmas with her family. For some reason, it reminded her of Lucas again, wondering what Christmas was like for him, in Switzerland, alone in his library of a house.

'I'd like that. And I'll be at college in between times. It'll give me a while to decide where I want to live.'

'Good. It's good that you're going back to college. You know, this week won't be any fun, but after the funeral we need to get back to living as normally as possible, and for you that means being twenty, being a student. The rest can wait; I'll take care of everything until such time as you want me to step aside.'

'Which is never. Thank God you're here, Simon. I don't know what I'd have done otherwise. I'd probably have sold everything.'

'No you wouldn't. You're tougher than you give yourself credit for.' He looked around casually. It was almost as if he expected to see a surveillance team listening in. 'This chap who protected you. You told them you didn't know who he was, his name or anything.'

'He told us it'd make life easier for him if we said that. We discussed it on the way to the consulate; it seemed the least we could do, really.'

Simon leaned back in his chair, clearly impressed, as he said, 'So you do know who he was! Tell me.'

'His name was Stephen Lucas. Dad hired him to watch us.'

He looked bemused, maybe a little shocked too, saying in response, 'Stephen Lucas. Is that what he called himself?'

'No, he called himself Lucas. He was about your age.'

'Amazing; I thought he'd retired. And he really wouldn't have been my first choice for close protection work.'

'You know him?' She answered the question almost immediately in her own mind, remembering that Lucas had told her he didn't know Simon.

'God, no! Heard of him. Unsavory type—had a vicious reputation as an enforcer, and as a contract killer.' An enforcer—she thought of that moment of rage with Chris, imagining it exploding into full-blown violence.

'I heard him say he'd killed people. And he killed three people to keep me alive—that's really all I need to know about him.'

'Absolutely. I should contact him, make sure he's been paid. Did he give you a contact number or an address?' She shook her head, wanting to keep the number he'd written in the book to herself. 'Oh well, I'm sure he'll be in touch with us if he needs the money. Was it his idea that you make a will out there?'

He seemed suspicious, worried perhaps, about what influence the mysterious Lucas might have had on her. Before she could answer, the boys' excited shouts burst out of the house and onto the lawn. Harry was carrying a tennis racket, George a ball.

They ran across to them, shouting, 'Ella, come and play with us.'

Simon raised his eyebrows, making clear he wouldn't offer an escape route.

'Let me guess: French cricket?' She was already standing but said to Simon, 'No, that was my idea. I've left everything to you, then to the boys.'

He looked reassured. 'Okay, let's have no more talk of death. We'll have enough of that in the next few weeks to last a lifetime.' She smiled, amused by his unfortunate choice of words, then joined the boys.

It was a relief to play games for a while. She'd wanted to hear about the business, to know something of the truth, but she was already sick of the details, wanting simply to forget it all and leave it in Simon's hands.

For half an hour or so, the only things that mattered were the minor disputes over whether George or Harry was out or not, each of them appealing to her like she was an omniscient umpire. Then Simon called her back to the house. As she approached, she could see two people behind him in the living room.

He sounded falsely cheerful. 'Police are here to have a little chat with you.'

'Okay.' She followed him in.

'This is my niece, Ella. This is—now let me get this right— Detective Inspector Graham Thorburn and Detective Sergeant Vicky Welsh.'

Thorburn was wearing a tie but no jacket, his hair slicked back in a high-maintenance style. He was probably about thirty, but Welsh looked not much older than Ella, her hair short, wearing a light skirt and a short loose blouse. She smiled at Ella even before they were introduced.

'Please, call us Graham and Vicky.' They shook hands.

'Probably best to use the library,' said Simon. 'Oddly enough, it's the only room the boys don't use as a racetrack.'

As he led them through, Graham Thorburn said, 'You don't mind if we speak to Ella alone?'

Ella wondered if it was a challenge, an attempt to rattle him, but Simon was calm. 'Not at all. Just give me a call if you need me for anything.' He left and they sat down, Ella on one sofa, the other two on the one facing it across a coffee table laid out with dusted but untroubled art books.

Vicky Welsh looked around the room and said, 'It's a beautiful house your uncle has here.'

'Yes, I suppose it is. Like an off-the-shelf Agatha Christie house.'

Her colleague laughed and, still smiling, said, 'Okay, Ella, if you feel up to it we'd just like to ask a few questions. If they seem intrusive it's only because we're determined to explore every channel in finding the person or persons who murdered your family.'

'Of course.'

'Good. First and most obvious then, can you think of anyone who might have had a grudge against your father or family or any reason why someone might have been moved to these actions?' Ella noticed that Vicky Welsh had taken a notebook out and was poised to record her answers. 'I want you even to recall if your father had any arguments in person or on the phone, if he ever seemed agitated in any way.'

'No.' She felt a little guilty offering such a short response to such a long question, but it was the truth. Still, she added, 'I can't remember the last time I saw him stressed about anything. It makes me wonder how well I really knew him.'

'Why? What makes you say that?' Clearly they were hoping she'd spill some of the truths she'd learned in the last day or two.

'Well, he must have been stressed if he was so afraid of me being kidnapped. Okay, I'm sure all parents worry, but not enough to hire a bodyguard.'

'Yes, I see. And you say this bodyguard never told you his name?'

'That's right. He told us we didn't need to know it. After seeing what he did we weren't in any mood to press him.'

'And you stayed at his house but you don't know where?' He sounded mildly skeptical.

'There was a small town nearby. I'd know the name if I saw it again—I just don't remember it.'

'That's okay.' Thorburn looked like he'd given up on the subject of Lucas, something in his manner suggesting he didn't believe a word of what she was saying about him. 'Your parents, were they happy? I mean, their marriage . . .'

'Yes, very.'

He smiled and said, 'What about your dad and your uncle—how was their relationship?'

'Good.'

'You never heard them argue about the business?' He was talking like Simon was a suspect and she wanted to ask if that was the case, holding off only because it seemed like the kind of clichéd question people always asked in TV crime dramas.

'I never heard them argue at all. And they never discussed business.'

'So you don't think your uncle was unhappy playing second fiddle to your dad?'

'Simon idolized my father.' She wanted to say more, to make clear how inappropriate she thought his line of questioning was, and how unfounded, but the shock of the implication had robbed her of eloquence. Perhaps he picked up on her indignation anyway, because he paused, they both looked a little embarrassed, and then the inspector subtly shifted gears.

'Our investigation's centered at the moment on your father's relatively complex business affairs. I'm sure you'll appreciate that we'll stand a much higher chance of finding the murderers if we have complete access . . .'

Ella cut him off, saying, 'You need to speak to my uncle about that.' It was her way of saying that she trusted Simon completely, more than she trusted them.

'But you'll give us your permission?' He was being vaguely confrontational and it irritated her. She didn't care about the business, but they seemed to care about it more than they did the murders.

'No, I'm sorry. That's up to Simon too.'

'But you *do* want us to find the people who killed your parents and brother.'

'Nice try.' She smiled, as if to make clear that she wouldn't be a pushover. That's clearly what they'd hoped, that they could use her innocence and her desperation. 'And while we're at it, I didn't much appreciate seeing newspaper headlines describing them as gangland executions. My father wasn't a gangster.'

Thorburn looked slightly hostile, his civility deserting him as he said, 'I can assure you, we've said nothing about that to the press.'

'Not directly, perhaps.'

'Not at all.' He stared at her, apparently mulling over whether or not it was worth asking any more questions. 'Well, I think that'll do for now. Thanks for your time.' The hostility was still there, perhaps disappointment too, and Ella felt like they were already repositioning her in their scheme of things. Then, on what sounded like a point of principle, he said, 'Even if your father had been a gangster, and I repeat that we have never implied that, we'd still be just as determined to find his killers.'

'Not as determined as I am.'

He nodded, not in agreement but by way of acknowledging that they were done, and said, 'I'm sorry for your loss.' He stood up. 'Your uncle has my number. If you think of anything, call me.'

Ella remained on the sofa after they'd gone, trying to take in what had happened. At some point in the last few days, between escorting her home and that interview, the police had shifted subtly along the axis from allies to adversaries. And as she defended her family's reputation, she felt more like a criminal herself, looking upon the authorities with an inbuilt mistrust.

There was a knock on the door and Vicky Welsh came back in, smiling.

'Hi. Look, sorry about Graham. The truth is, somebody in the police probably did drop a hint to the press. It's a way of telling the public not to worry, but it isn't fair on you.' She handed her a piece of paper and said, 'That's my direct line and my mobile. If you need to talk to me or find out how things are going, just give me a call.'

'Thanks.'

'Don't mention it. Keep hanging in there.' She walked away but stopped again and turned before reaching the door. 'Ella . . .' She hesitated, as if unsure how to put her thoughts into words, then said simply, 'Just be careful.'

'I will.'

The police clearly had nothing to go on. They were thrashing around, looking at Simon as a suspect, getting hung up on the business side of things. Within a few weeks they'd probably think she'd been behind it herself.

Perhaps it was too early to dismiss their efforts, but she couldn't bear the possibility of no one being caught. Someone out there right now had gone to their home and killed her family, and men had come for her in Italy, and someone out there had ordered those deaths, had paid the gunmen.

It filled her with poison to think that the people who'd done this were walking free, getting on with their lives. Within days she'd have to attend the funeral for the world she'd known, and in the back of her mind, beyond all the confused layers of grief, she'd be thinking of those persons unknown, laughing, eating, drinking.

Her dad hadn't been a gangster, but right now she'd have forgiven him even that, because her own heart was full of more violence than his could have mustered. And that scared her, because if the police failed to bring anyone to justice she could see no outlet for that violence, and no one who could exorcise it from her.

Chapter Eight

She kept a book by her side, ready to fool anyone who came in, knowing how they'd react if they thought she was just sitting there, looking out at the rain. She wasn't sure what she was meant to be doing instead, but there seemed a general consensus that it wasn't good for her to dwell on things. Her family was in the ground now and it was time for her to move on, to put all this unpleasantness aside. That's how easy it was meant to be.

And yet if anything, she felt worse than she had around the time of the funeral; at least then there had been arrangements and decisions to make, things to take her mind off the blank horror of what had happened. Now she didn't even have the distraction of the boys, who'd been spirited off to Lucy's parents for a week.

So she sat in silence, looking out at the rain that had been falling for the best part of two days. In her better moments she thought of the drive with Lucas, through similar weather to the sanctuary of his house. Most of the time, though, her mind was lost in the featureless wastes, latching on wherever it could—a burst of self-pity, a nostalgic recollection and, increasingly, a gnawing desire to destroy the people responsible, a desire that was hollow, eating away at her insides because she didn't even know who those people were.

She was beginning to hate the police for failing to make any progress. Eventually, she'd undoubtedly begin to hate herself too, because she was still alive, still capable of seeing justice done and yet she was doing nothing; her inertia felt like a betrayal.

She heard a door close downstairs and then low voices. She couldn't hear who it was, but guessed they were discussing her. They often seemed to talk about her in quiet, concerned voices like that, like she was ill or on suicide watch.

The voices stopped, and for a while she strained to hear more noise. There was nothing and then a knock at her door that startled her. She picked her book up quickly and called out nonchalantly for them to come in. She kept her eyes on the book as the door opened, but glanced at the reflection in the rain-darkened window to see who it was.

The figure she saw there startled her again and she jumped up, her feelings scattering in confusion. She felt like an amnesiac, believing this was the man she loved but not quite sure where she'd hidden the memory of that love inside herself.

Chris almost ran to her, put his arms around her and held her tight. She dropped the book and held him back, a reflexive response to the warmth and touch of his body. He whispered in her ear, about missing her, apologizing for not having come sooner, the reasons he hadn't been at the funeral.

She stroked his hair. 'It's okay, I understand.' She broke away long enough to kiss him and said then, 'Shall we sit down?'

He looked troubled, as if she'd said something strange or as if he mistrusted something about her appearance, but he smiled and said, 'Of course.'

They talked for a while like people from another age, making polite inquiries. She could tell he was finding it hard work, but she could see no way through to the relaxed conversation she knew they should be having.

Finally, as if hitting upon an escape, Chris said, 'I was talking to your uncle and one of the policemen about the possibility of us going away for a few days.' She wasn't conscious of reacting but he appeared to pick up on something and added, 'I don't mean right now. Later in the summer. We could just go somewhere quiet, relax.'

'Somewhere like Montecatini?'

'That's why we should go somewhere, to get rid of that association.'

She glanced out at the rain. If the police found the killers, she could imagine going somewhere with Chris, but they wouldn't find them. She wouldn't be safe and she wouldn't be at peace, no matter where they went.

'The police don't know what they're doing.' He looked confused, so she smiled a little and said, 'If the police find them, then I'll go. I just don't like the idea of . . .'

'I know. But if the police find them, you'll consider it?'

She nodded and he kissed her and held her again, whispering once more how he'd missed her but with a different meaning this time, his hand spelling it out, marking its territory across her body, finally securing itself to her left breast, kneading the flesh.

He'd never known how to handle her breasts. A couple of times she'd tried to offer some gentle guidance but had given up, accepting the lack of pleasure and occasional discomfort, telling herself he made up for it in other ways.

He released her suddenly, backing away as he said, 'What's up?'

'What do you mean?'

'I mean you seem uncomfortable, rigid.'

'Sorry.'

'I don't want an apology. I just wanna know what's up. You're not upset with me?' She looked him in the eye, trying to remind herself who this was. She still loved him, but it was as if he were visiting her in a maximum-security prison, a layer of impenetrable glass between them, with no way to convey to him how it felt to be on her side.

'I can't think straight. It's like you're touching me and I can't feel anything, nothing, just . . . I just need more time.'

He looked hesitant, careful. 'Your aunt said you were on medication. You think maybe you should get them to up the dose?' She looked at him in disbelief.

'You want me loved up so we can fuck?'

'That isn't what I meant.'

'Chris, I'm flushing the pills.'

It was his turn to look shocked.

'I thought the doctor said you were depressed.'

'Of course I'm depressed. Someone killed my family. I'm depressed and I'm angry and I'm full of hate—that's how I should feel.'

'Why? What are you gonna gain from bringing yourself down?'

She saw no point in explaining. Everyone wanted her to be happy; that was the lie of their age, that being happy was the goal. Take the pills, be happy, forget that the sky had been torn from the world this summer. But she was a country at war, its territory invaded, citizens slaughtered, fighting for its survival. How could she explain that to Chris?

Finally she put her hand on his and said, 'I just need you to wait for me. A few more weeks, that's all.'

He shook his head.

'No.' Her confusion obviously showed because he said, 'You need me right now, whether you know it or not, and if you can't accept that on trust, I can't see what difference a few weeks will make.'

She knew what he wanted: to have her back the way she'd been. He wanted her to take the pills and get better, to wind the clock back to that moment in Montecatini before Lucas had crossed the street and killed two men for her. And like a dull distant bell sounding, she sensed what she'd feared from the beginning: that it was over between them.

She desperately wanted Chris to accept her for who she was now but she feared he'd always be waiting on her recovery. And he'd never understand that she wasn't damaged but in fact more complete, possessed of the truth of how the world really was.

'If the police find someone . . .'

'What if they don't?'

'I don't know.' He stood up. He was leaving already and a part of her was relieved, but even so, she couldn't believe that he was giving up so quickly. 'Why did you come here?'

It was the wrong question and not what she'd meant to say, but he said, 'Because I missed you, and because I thought you might need me.' She felt bad and was willing herself to stand up, to hold him, but he looked hurt, rejected.

'I'll start taking the pills.' She didn't mean it, but she wanted to offer him something. 'And we'll go somewhere like you said, in September.'

'Do you want me to stay now?' It wasn't an offer, more a demand for clarification, her hesitation all the response he needed. 'I'll be at home all summer.' He left.

She was exhausted. She didn't know how to speak to anyone anymore. Maybe she'd write to him and when they got back to college things would be different.

She heard voices below, doors, the faint sound of a car starting and pulling away from the front of the house. Equally distant in her own head, a voice registered the effort he'd gone to, driving all the way over here to see her, intent on staying perhaps, helping her through this, an effort she'd repaid with rejection.

There was another gentle knock at the door. She didn't need to look at the reflection to know it was Simon. He walked over and put his hand on her shoulder.

She lifted her own hand, clasping it around his fingers as she said, 'Sorry.'

'No, I am. I thought it might cheer you up.' He paused before saying, 'They wouldn't have wanted you to be like this.' The phrase rang false somehow, like something he'd heard in a schmaltzy TV movie and felt uncomfortable repeating.

'Wouldn't they? How do you know?' She turned to look at him. He looked embarrassed, even afraid. 'When I die I hope I leave at least one person as heartbroken as I am now. I want people to be sad. I want my life to have meant something.'

He smiled a little. 'We agreed there'd be no more talk of death.'

'Just give me this summer. One summer to grieve for a lost family—it's not too much to ask, is it?'

He shook his head. 'Of course not. But think about going away with Chris in September. Aim for it. It'll do you good.' She nodded and he smiled again and closed the door softly behind him. She felt like screaming, like she was the only person who could see what had happened.

She looked at the telephone and suddenly thought of Lucas. It was absurd that his was the only phone number she possessed that still meant anything, that was still connected to the world she inhabited. And yet what would she say to him if she called? He'd care nothing that she was at a low point. Even the fact that she was still alive would probably be of only marginal interest to him.

For all that, though, the reason she didn't pick up the phone was more practical. Lucas was her fallback position, her last resort, and as bad as things seemed, she wanted to keep him in reserve for the day they got worse. Lucas didn't know it, but she was counting on him more than anybody.

Chapter Nine

It couldn't be her. This girl had dark hair, but he sensed that she was going to the house, and sure enough she stopped and rang the bell—one of her friends, perhaps, a pretty girl.

He trained the lens on the door but the angle was no good, and whoever opened it stayed out of shot as the girl stepped inside. He was desperate to get in that house and see its domestic topography, Madeleine and their daughter, a husband perhaps, other kids.

He couldn't imagine her parents still lived there. They'd probably made way for her, moved to the place in the country. Thinking of them made him nostalgic, remembering how much he'd liked them, more memories of Madeleine spilling in on the back of that thought.

He wanted to see her again, not with any hope of rekindling the past, just to tell her he'd finally changed, or retired at least. It probably wouldn't mean anything to her, though, and maybe she'd be right not to care what he'd done with his life.

He wasn't even certain how much he really had changed. He could think through his conversations with Ella Hatto and convince himself it was time for him to reconnect with the world, but maybe it was all just self-delusion.

After all, this was his idea of reconnecting with his former girl-friend and daughter, sitting in a car a hundred yards from their house with a camera and a telephoto lens. He was stalking his own daughter and could think of no other way to get close to her; that's how far removed he was from normal life.

He was beginning to think he should just give up and go back to the hotel, or even back to Switzerland, when the door opened again. He trained the camera on it in time to see the girl with dark hair come out, then another girl, the familiarity of her appearance giving him a jolt of nervous excitement. His muscles weakened so suddenly that he had to lean on the wheel to stop the camera from shaking.

She was blonde, her hair quite short, whereas Madeleine had always worn hers long. Otherwise, it could have been Madeleine at fourteen. And that made him happy, because she had nothing of him about her; she was like her mother and she was beautiful.

They were walking away from him now and he felt a surge of panic. For a second, he wasn't sure what to do, whether to sit and wait or to follow them. The indecision was only momentary, though, because he wasn't staking out the house; he was there to see his daughter.

He put the camera on the floor deep in the passenger well, picked up his book and crossed the street. He walked quickly at first, but adopted a more casual gait once he was certain of not losing them.

He was close enough to hear their voices and their laughter, and occasionally they'd look at each other and he'd get a glimpse of her face and another jolt of nerves, fearing she'd turn and see him. A part of him wanted her to turn. He wanted her to throw a glance at the man far behind and then stop, snagged, knowing instinctively who it was.

He followed them to a cafe but didn't go in, realizing that, even in Paris, sitting reading an English paperback might mark him out. He bought a copy of *Le Monde*, waited as long as he could, then walked into the cafe.

The place was busy but there were enough tables free for him to choose one that gave him a clear view of her face without being too close. A young waiter arrived at their table and they spoke to him with the haughty condescension of rich kids, borderline rude. That disappointed him; he wanted her to be more like Ella Hatto, someone who hadn't known she was rich and who was balanced and polite.

Possibly they'd been play-acting, though. The waiter said something back to them and they both laughed loudly enough to draw the stares of other customers. Then they looked embarrassed that they'd attracted attention like that, and seemed more natural afterwards.

Lucas ordered a coffee from another waiter and watched as the girls got their drinks. They were chatty and friendly with their waiter now, maybe even knew him; it shouldn't have mattered but Lucas was relieved all the same.

He got his own coffee and started his pretense of reading the newspaper, a token effort because neither she nor anyone else was looking in his direction. He took it for granted now, even resented it, but in the past his ability to be inconspicuous had amazed him. He'd done a hit in a crowded restaurant in Hamburg, and not one person had given an accurate description of him afterwards. They'd even disagreed—tall, short, blond hair, red hair, glasses, sunglasses, definitely not wearing glasses at all. It was like they'd all been hypnotized and told to forget him.

Lucas had been watching for ten minutes or so when they were joined by another girl and two boys. The girl and one of the boys were clearly brother and sister, the third the sister's boyfriend. There was more banter with the waiter.

Maybe this was where they came to hang out. He thought briefly about doing the same each day, but in a cafe like that even his face would become familiar. He'd take it easy. When they left, he'd stroll back to the car, then go back to the hotel. And he'd go to the house again in the morning, hopeful of catching a glimpse of Madeleine herself.

Then he'd decide how to approach the girl: in person or by letter. Madeleine would intercept a letter, of course, but he could get around that. He'd wait until he saw her friend approaching and give her the letter, ask her to give it to—who? The least he had to do was find out her name.

He grew annoyed now that he was sitting so far away. Yet their voices were just audible and he strained to pick up one of them addressing her by name. He could hear only a jumble of French vocabulary, though, all vaguely familiar but meaningless. And as he watched he became mesmerized by her face, her expressions— smiles, thoughtful glances, a playfully knitted brow. It made him sad to think he hadn't seen those expressions mapped out across her childhood.

Those years were lost, all the years when he might have read stories to her, seen her through the milestones: birthdays and swimming and riding bikes, the things he imagined fathers doing. But she'd done those things without him and he'd killed probably a hundred people during the blameless span of her life.

His eyes shifted briefly and he twitched nervously as he realized the brother was looking at him, a bemused look on his face. The kid leaned over to say something to the others and Lucas lifted his paper, just enough to obscure his face.

He couldn't believe he'd been spotted looking at her like that, annoyed by the interpretation they were bound to put on it. His heart was lurching, knowing that they were probably looking across at him right now, trying to get a glimpse of his face.

Having seen the confident, proprietary air they'd had with the waiter, he couldn't even be certain they wouldn't come over. He laughed edgily, struck by the irony of his cowering behind a newspaper in fear of five smart-looking fourteen-year-olds. And he sat like that for five minutes or so before leaving, casually keeping his face turned away from them.

He still felt an adrenaline buzz as he walked back to the car. He'd seen her. She was beautiful, someone with nice friends, popular. And with the adrenaline came a longing, a consuming need for this to be a beginning, not an end.

It was selfish. He couldn't imagine how she felt or if she even knew about him. For all he knew, her life was happy and full, and his appearance might be as shattering a blow as a death in the family. He was thinking only of himself, he knew that, but he had to find a way to her. Suddenly, with all the power of a spiritual revelation, he couldn't see a reason for being alive otherwise.

After dinner that night he sat in the bar with his book, his newfound optimism making him want to be around other people, even if it didn't stretch to actually wanting to talk to them. He hadn't been there long when an elderly lady sat at the next table. Lucas pretended not to see her smile as she sat down.

He heard her order a Bellini, her accent Scottish, Edinburgh maybe, and was conscious of another brief exchange when the drink was delivered. He concentrated on his book and was surprised when he heard her speak a few minutes later.

'Excuse me for intruding, but is it your first time?' He looked up, assuming that someone else had sat down, and caught the full force of her smiling, inquisitive stare. He had no choice but to answer that most banal of travelers' questions.

'Not my first time in Paris. First time in this hotel.'

'No, dear, that's not what I meant at all.' She smiled, pointing at the book. 'I mean, is it your first time reading *Pride and Prejudice*?'

'Oh, I see.' He laughed. 'Yes, it is. Someone recommended Jane Austen to me and I'm hooked. *Mansfield Park, Northanger Abbey, Persuasion*—that's my favorite so far.'

'It's mine too. Quite a delightful book. It's poignant too, of course, when one thinks of it in terms of Jane Austen's own life, but life-affirming nevertheless. Don't you think? It's never too late to make amends for the wrongs of the past.'

He hadn't given much thought to why he liked the book, but maybe it was that—the hope it offered for the future, no matter how blighted the past.

'You really believe that, that it's never too late?'

'I do indeed. I've seen it, just as I've seen people live their lives full of regret, never dreaming there might still be time to do something about it. What a sad way to be going on.'

'I suppose it is.'

She smiled. 'And tell me, dear, are you on your own here? That's a terrible shame.'

'I'm used to traveling alone. It's a business trip.'

'Even so.'

He wasn't sure she believed him and didn't want to be pressed, so he deflected her concern by saying, 'Are you not traveling alone yourself?'

'Goodness, no. My husband's taken an early night after rather overdoing it last night. And my son and his wife have taken a night cruise on the Seine. Maybe you'll meet them; I'm expecting them back any time now.'

'Actually, I'm turning in shortly. I have a busy day tomorrow.' The conversation had been pleasant enough, but he didn't much want to meet the next generation, people who might be more inclined to ask him what he did and whether he had a family, and wouldn't he join them for a drink or dinner—it was all too much contact.

'Oh. Well, never mind.' Again she had that look about her as though she'd seen right through him. 'Thank you for chatting anyway.'

'No, thank you.'

'Thank Jane Austen.' He smiled and took his leave, pleased to have concluded the conversation before they'd exchanged names.

He felt good about himself afterwards too. It would have been nothing to most people but to engage in any spontaneous social interaction was a departure for him. And he felt good about the things she'd said, filling him with a determination to follow the only logical course: to speak to Madeleine.

He'd changed in fifteen years and she would have, too. He'd always imagined her holding on to all that anger and bitterness, but time would have mollified her; it had to have. He'd talk to her and she'd see that he was someone she could deal with again.

The next morning he was less confident. He'd found a space a little closer to the house and watched as the sun slowly heated up the street. His aim was to wait until the girl went out, and then to go over and ring the bell.

That was the idea, but elderly ladies and the works of Jane Austen were one thing; walking back into his past was another. In the harsh morning light, he couldn't help but think Madeleine would see his return as just another betrayal of trust, one that would bring back whatever memories she'd buried.

He didn't know how he'd ever thought that renouncing his former life would be enough for her. And now he feared that if he walked over to that house it might be to have the door close in his face forever.

He'd arrived at about twenty past nine and he'd started to think they might all have gone out early or even left the city, but just after ten a woman in her twenties came out and walked up the street past his car.

She was carrying a folder under one arm and looked like a student. Without much to go on other than instinct and the way she looked, Lucas reckoned on her being a music teacher. And because of her age he came to the further unfounded conclusion that there were younger kids in the house.

Madeleine would have had their daughter learn an instrument—the piano, he hoped, like she had—but at fourteen, her tuition wouldn't be entrusted to someone so young. If she was a music teacher, then some younger child of Madeleine's had just spent an hour practicing the violin or piano, whatever.

Locked out of those details, he had an exile-driven curiosity. For the next half an hour, he built pictures of the life being lived behind that door, populating his memory of the grand house with various imagined families, all of them with Madeleine at the centre.

Then a car pulled up and sounded its horn. He trained the camera on the driver but couldn't see beyond the reflection on the windshield. Shifting his aim toward the door, he caught the girl coming out, smiling, jumping into the back of the car.

He put the camera down as the car moved in his direction. He took in the driver, a middle-aged woman, and then the two girls in the back. As they talked to each other, he could see his daughter's face. For a moment, it looked as if she were looking directly at him, her smile for him.

He got out of the car without thinking what he was doing, walked over to the house and rang the bell. Almost immediately he heard a commotion inside. He was right about the younger child: there were excitable shouts nearby followed by a mildly chastising adult voice growing in volume as it approached from deep inside the house. The door opened and he was faced by a maid.

'Hello. Do you speak English?'

The answer was clear. She gave him a look as if to suggest he was being intentionally awkward, and then said something that he took to be a request to wait there. As she closed the door, he caught a glimpse of a little blond boy in long shorts and a T-shirt. He was peering out but as soon as he made eye contact with Lucas he ran off into the house.

When the door opened again, Madeleine was standing in front of him, wearing a simple red summer dress, her hair pulled back loosely into a ponytail. Her figure was still perfect, her face as youthful as it was in the one picture he had of her.

He was ambushed by how beautiful she was, no less so than he had been all those years before. For a second, he couldn't speak and, whatever shock or emotion his appearance had inflicted on her, she didn't speak either. It was as if she were trying to remember what her response was meant to be to this situation, one she must surely have imagined, even planned for.

'Hello, Madeleine. I waited till she'd gone out.' The spell was broken, the sound of his voice apparently all she'd needed to remember how they stood.

'Big of you. What are you doing here, Luke?'

'It's good to see you, Madeleine.' The child called her and she automatically closed the door behind her before responding, her tone pleasant, indulgent. He could imagine her being a good mother. He knew this wouldn't go well, though—that closing of the door, an expression of her desire to keep him even from her other child, upon whom he had no claims.

She turned back to him and said again, 'What are you doing here?'

The only route open now was directness.

'I want to see her. I know I made a promise but I want to see her, talk to her. And maybe she wants to meet me, find out who I am.'

'We made an agreement. *You* agreed not to see her, specifically to protect her from the knowledge of who you are, the kind of person you are. And what, now because of a selfish whim you want to expose her to all of that?'

'Selfish, maybe, but it's no whim. I changed my life, Madeleine. Not soon enough, I'll admit, but I changed it.'

Her tone was softer but still insistent as she said, 'Our lives have changed too, Luke. We're a family, happy, settled. It's the wrong time for this. I'm asking you to go away—not for me, for Isabelle.'

'Isabelle?' He choked on the word, his throat tightening with emotion. He couldn't believe it overwhelmed him so much just to hear her name for the first time, to be able to say it, the three syllables like some perfectly formed haiku.

Madeleine appeared not to notice. 'Yes, her name's Isabelle, and she's happy, and not curious. Besides, she doesn't speak English, only 'please' and 'thank you,' 'hello.' I'm assuming you still don't speak French?' He shook his head, sensing that beneath her gentle tone was real malice and bitterness. He could imagine Madeleine steering her away from English all these years, knowing the barrier that language would place between them. 'So tell me, Luke, what good would come from a meeting, what good for Isabelle?'

She was right. The girl was clearly happy, and how could he say this wasn't a whim when in fourteen years it had never crossed his mind to learn her native language? How could he not have thought of that? He couldn't even think of anything to say in response to Madeleine, could only nod, dejected.

'Please don't come back, Luke. Promise me.' He didn't want to promise. He wanted her to ask him in, to tell him about her life. He wanted to hold her again, to help her out of that light summer dress, to feel her skin against his. It was never too late.

'I'll be out of Paris by this afternoon.' He turned away and then heard her call behind him.

'Promise me.' He didn't respond, just kept walking to the car, and by the time he got there and looked back, the door was closed.

He couldn't understand how a promise from him could be of any worth to her now. But at the moment, he couldn't understand anything. What was the point? If there was never going to be a way back, what was the point of any of it?

Chapter Ten

Throughout the dark summer, this was what she'd focused on to keep sane and yet, just one week into term, she knew she shouldn't have come back, that it was too soon. She'd thought this would be a return to something, but it was like a glaring compare-and-contrast exercise—the person she was now against the person who'd left for the vacation three months before.

It was five o'clock. She'd just come out of a lecture on the Romantic poets and was part of the damp, twilit migration that filled the campus, students heading to final lectures or back to their halls. She blended in well enough, but she felt like she was carrying a virus that none of the people around her were aware of.

There was definitely a sickness within her. Her blood was unstable, always running too hot or too cold, filling her with violent urges or rendering her too fragile and lifeless to leave her bed. And she could no longer cope with society, with small talk, with friends who pretended to show an interest but who just wanted ammunition for gossip.

She spotted Chris walking towards her. He was the main reason she'd come back and the main reason she should have stayed away. He'd written a letter a week after visiting her at Simon's so she'd known it was over, but she'd still believed that if she came back to college they might be able to pick things up again, at least remain friends.

She'd gone to his room on her second day back, but he hadn't even been able to look her in the eye, his body tense as soon as she touched him. And he'd kept using that same phrase, 'like I said in my letter,' as if the sentiments he'd expressed there had been beyond his control, as if he had no choice but to abide by them.

She wasn't sure what to say to him now, and rehearsed the possibilities in her head, deciding that a casual hello would be best, something that showed how relaxed she was and that she understood things were different. She became less confident as they neared each other, but at the crucial moment he denied her the opportunity to say anything by bowing his head and looking at the floor.

Ella was sure he'd seen her and she stopped, shocked and infuriated, and confused because she couldn't understand what she'd done to deserve such coldness. She'd blamed herself earlier in the summer, but she'd been wrong—Chris had failed *her* and she hated him for it.

She looked at the back of his head as he walked away and felt the rage building up inside her. Before she knew what she was doing, she was pursuing him through the crowd. She grabbed him by the arm and pulled him around. He looked momentarily afraid and then angry.

'Don't you dare ignore me!'

Chris almost screamed in response, 'What's your fucking problem?'

A dozen answers spilled into her head at once, none of them strong enough or big enough to counter the cruelty of his simple four-word jibe. He'd treated her appallingly, abandoning her when she needed him most, but with a few careless words he could dismiss her as some obsessive former girlfriend and cast himself as the victim. It wasn't fair.

'I don't have any problems. Remember?'

'You need to see a shrink.'

She laughed scathingly and said, 'You can't even bring yourself to smile and say hello, but I'm the one who needs a shrink.'

He didn't respond and a moment later he shook his head a little and started to turn away. It incensed her that he was refusing to take her on or even acknowledge her argument. She wouldn't be ignored. Furious, she pulled him back by the arm again and, before he could speak, slapped him hard across the face.

He raised his own hand in reflex and looked set to strike her back, but stopped himself. Her hand was stinging and his cheek had reddened almost immediately, his right eye looking watery. It had clearly hurt, but he still denied her what she most wanted, dropping his hand and turning again, walking away into the crowd.

Ella became aware for the first time that a few people had stopped and were staring at her now. When she met their gazes, they moved on quickly. She too continued on her way, energy draining from her as if she were wounded.

By the time she got back to her hall the anger had subsided, but she felt weak. She decided to check the kitchen—if no one was in there yet she'd cook something. There were two people making dinner, though, Scarlett and Al, so she made for her locker and got bread and jam to take back to her room.

Scarlett had been a friend in the first year, less so since, and gave her a cheery hello as she walked in. She hardly knew Al, but he was a prick and had made crass jokes all week about the stuff that had been in the papers over the summer.

As she closed her locker, he said, 'Ella, have you been in my room?' She turned and looked at him, waiting for the punch line. 'I think you left your horse head in my bed.'

'That was almost funny, Al.'

He turned to Scarlett and said, 'She smiled—I'm safe for another day.'

Scarlett looked embarrassed and tried to shush him.

Ella was irritated by Al Brown, but at least he was upfront. She despised Scarlett and all the others because they made a less than convincing show of being tactful and supportive, and all the while, she knew they were talking about her, had heard them whispering outside her door or been met by a sudden silence as she entered the kitchen.

Back in her room, she made sandwiches and wondered what she had to do to get her life back. She had to leave college, that was a given, and to accept that she could never go back to being the person she was before. Whatever life she fashioned for herself, it would have to be one that incorporated the baggage of the last three months.

Maybe she also needed to take things into her own hands. It had been an easy escape, shirking her responsibility by convincing herself that other people were looking into the murders. But the resulting guilt and frustration had almost certainly played a crucial role in bringing her down, and were no doubt key ingredients in the anger she felt constantly bubbling beneath the surface.

She looked at the clock. It was nearly five-thirty. She reached into the drawer for a piece of paper and rang the number on it. The answer came so quickly that she was thrown for a moment, the reason for her call not yet fully worked out.

'Hi, Vicky. It's Ella Hatto here. You said I could call you.' There was a pause. Vicky Welsh had probably dealt with a hundred crimes since their meeting and it seemed to take her a second or two to place Ella.

When she spoke, though, it was with an urgency, as if she feared Ella might hang up, 'Ella, how have you been? What can I do for you?'

'I just wanted to know if there's been any progress.'

'Uh, we are still exploring some lines of inquiry, but I have to be honest, we don't have anything concrete.' There was another pause before she proceeded gingerly. 'And of course, you're not really helping yourself, Ella.'

'What do you mean?'

'You know what I mean. The clues to your family's killers have got to be hidden somewhere within your dad's business dealings. Now I know that some of his business in the past was a little colorful, but I promise you, that's not what we want to investigate. We don't want to tarnish your dad's name, just to find evidence that might point to his murderer.'

'I can't.' She wanted to, but she couldn't. She didn't want to betray Simon, and she was fearful that, despite Vicky Welsh's promises, her dad's name *would* be tarnished one way or another, with revelations this time, not just innuendo.

'Would you at least talk about it with your uncle? Maybe ask him why he's so determined on being uncooperative?'

'You don't understand. I . . .'

'Don't decide now. Think about it and we'll speak again.'

'Okay.'

'We're still on your side, you know.'

'I know. Thanks.'

She hung up the phone and thought back over their brief, unsatisfactory conversation—she wasn't helping herself, she was hindering their search for the killers. She was convinced that if her dad were with her now, he'd tell her not to fall for it, to listen to Simon.

Maybe he'd also tell her that the time had come to call Lucas. She could imagine her dad talking to her now, using the tone he reserved for fundamental truths about how life should be lived— always ask for an upgrade, always ask for a discount, never leave a drink unattended, buy property, don't rent it, trust Lucas, never trust the police.

She wouldn't betray Simon or allow them to dismantle the business her dad had built, certainly not for the kind of justice they'd hand down if they ever did find the killers. At least if Lucas found them, he'd have no qualms about delivering the punishment they deserved.

She took the copy of *The Nibelungenlied* off the shelf, the bookmark still in place at the point she'd reached when Lucas had broken the news. Before meeting him she'd never seen a gun, never seen someone killed, never seen a dead person; his entire world had been alien to her, and she knew that if she took up his offer of help she'd be embracing it and becoming a part of it. But it was a compact she was willing to make if it helped her achieve this one thing.

She turned to the page where he'd written and without hesitating, she dialed the number. It took a while to connect and then rang for a long time before the phone picked up. There was silence and Ella waited for the answering machine to kick in before realizing that there wasn't one, that Lucas had picked up the phone but remained silent.

It seemed typical of him and she smiled as she said, 'It's Ella Hatto here.'

'Are you in trouble?'

'No, no.'

'That's good.' There was a pause. She could sense him struggling to think of something to say, something other than asking her why she was calling. 'So how have you been?'

'Okay. I'm back at college.'

'Good.'

'Actually, not okay. I thought I could get back to normal but I can't, not until the people who did this are caught, and that's not looking likely any time soon.'

'Why did you call me?' The question was okay now, loaded, a suggestion in the tone of his voice that he knew but wanted confirmation.

'I want you to help me find them. I'll pay you.'

'No. No payments—I retired.'

There was one of his pauses, even more disconcerting on the phone. She waited for him to continue and when she realized he wasn't going to, she said, 'But you will help me find them? I thought you could . . .' He interrupted.

'Don't say any more. What room are you in?'

'I'm in Radstone Hall on the campus. Room D76.'

'I'll be there as soon as I can.' Another pause, but after a few seconds he added, 'I'm glad you called. Bye.'

'Bye.'

She smiled to herself as she hung up the phone. What had her world come to, that speaking to Lucas could leave her feeling more calm and at peace than she'd felt in months? During most of the time she'd spent in his company, he'd seemed like the manifestation of her problems. But for all his failings, he'd been her salvation, he'd been true, and now he'd be the weapon with which she would avenge her family.

Part Three

Chapter Eleven

He didn't see much of the campus from the taxi, just a general overview, a sprawl of modern buildings lost in the rain. Even so, the sight of it produced a twitch of excitement in him; he'd never been to a college before, and it was the one thing he regretted about his youth, that the opportunity had never been available to him.

He ran the twenty yards from the taxi to the archway that led into Radstone Hall, an irregular quad with flower beds and picnic benches, abandoned and wet. There was a building map on the wall of the archway and he stopped to look at it.

Two girls came out of a doorway and passed him before one stopped. 'Are you lost? Can I help?'

He smiled. These were the kind of people to be found at college. 'Thanks. I'm looking for D76.'

'That staircase over there. Third floor.'

He thanked her and walked on. There was another short burst of cold rain, and as he ascended through the floors, a collage of noise, music, voices—all people unseen, a tantalizing suggestion of the hermetic world he was skirting. He felt like a ghost, enviously looking out on a future it could never know.

Ella's door was closed and there was no response. He strolled along the corridor, the only room open apparently unoccupied, and into a mess of a kitchen where a guy was sitting on an easy chair. He didn't seem to be doing anything and for a moment he looked expectantly at the opening door, losing interest once he saw Lucas.

'Hi, I'm looking for Ella Hatto.'

'Thanks for letting me know.' The response and the tone caught Lucas off guard; he couldn't remember the last time anyone had spoken to him with that kind of insolence, and he was annoyed because it was happening here, in a place where he didn't want to think badly of anyone.

He walked further into the room so that he was only a few feet away. Lucas noticed now that there was a bad smell in there, like food waste, and he couldn't understand how anyone could sit there and not be bothered by it.

Giving it a second try, he said, 'Do you know where she might be, where I might find her?'

'Probably being a miserable bitch somewhere.'

'Excuse me?'

'Excused.' Lucas was still finding it difficult to take on board how rude and arrogant this guy was, and how stupid. It was shattering his whole image of academia that there could be people like this within it.

'You should be careful who you're rude to.'

'Did I ask for advice? What, am I meant to be scared? Are you one of her drug-dealing cohorts or something? Well, I'm not impressed, so why don't you just fuck off and leave me alone.'

It wasn't good. This was why he lived the way he did, removed from the world, because it was tough becoming the person he wanted to be when so many other people were this unpleasant.

Lucas smacked him hard in the face, not hard enough to do any real damage but enough to knock him off the chair. It was clear from his expression that the punch had come out of the blue, that the guy had no idea what he might have done to invite it.

He scuttled clumsily across the floor, clutching his face, and backed into the wall.

'What the fuck was that!'

'That was a punch. And this is a gun, pointing at your head; lucky for you I'm trying to renounce violence.'

He started towards the door, but the guy shouted after him, saying, 'I'll have you fucking crucified for this!'

Lucas turned at the door and said, 'I just knocked you across the room for cheeking me. You really want to take this further?'

He checked Ella's door again on the way out, then found a coffee bar. He sat at a small table in the corner, soaking up the atmosphere, the small huddles of students, surges of laughter and conversation. These too seemed like good people and Lucas felt comforted, reassured.

He went back half an hour later. Ella's door was still closed but he could hear movement inside and when he knocked, she shouted for him to come in. She appeared to be a good way into the process of packing her room up. She looked around as he closed the door behind him and froze midway through folding the duvet.

'I'd begun to think you might not come.'

She didn't look well. Or maybe it wasn't that she looked ill, but that she looked hardened. He couldn't quite pin it down and then he became conscious that he was staring. He turned his attention to the room and said, 'Looks like I'm just in time.'

She looked around and said, 'Yeah, I'm leaving, until next year at least.' She put the duvet down on the bed, adding, 'I can still offer you a coffee, though.'

'No, I'm good.' He pointed at the chair. 'May I?'

'Of course.' She sat on the edge of the bed. 'Thank you for coming.'

'I read *Persuasion*.'

She looked confused by the comment. These were the parts of conversations he still found difficult, the decorative borders around the real business.

'Oh, good. Did you enjoy it?'

'Yes. Not life-changing or anything but a good book. I read some more of hers too.' She smiled politely, maybe because she hadn't read any more Austen herself and didn't know how to respond, maybe just because this wasn't how people talked to each other. 'You want me to find the people who killed your family.'

She nodded, looking relieved.

'And if I find them?'

'I wanna see whoever it is sent to prison. I want justice.'

Probably the biggest favor he could do her right now would be to get up and walk out. She wanted the truth of what had happened to her family, he could understand that, but she thought it could all be neatly sealed up, that justice would be done if only the evidence could be put before the system.

'I can find them but I'm telling you straight, you won't make anything stick. And even if you did, the justice handed out wouldn't be enough, not for what they did to you.'

'I don't understand.' That looked like an understatement, her expression one of complete bewilderment. 'You're saying you can find them but it's pointless.'

'It isn't pointless but you have to be true to yourself about what you really want. If the person who killed your parents and brother was standing in front of you right now, what would you want? Truthfully, what would you want?'

120

He didn't say any more, giving her time to think, hoping for her sake, and maybe for his, too, that she'd come down on the tougher side of the fence. He was determined to let her know exactly where the seductive pull of revenge would take her.

A knock on the door broke her introspective spell. She pointed for him to stand by the cupboard, out of sight from the doorway. He moved, and listened as she opened the door.

'Hello, Brian.'

'Hello, Ella.' It was an older man's voice. 'I'm really sorry to bother you with this but you know I have to check these things out.'

'Of course. What is it?' Lucas knew immediately what this call was about and couldn't believe the guy from the kitchen had been stupid enough to report it after what he'd said to him. He felt like killing him just as a service to the gene pool.

'Al Brown claims one of your visitors assaulted him and uh, well, uh . . .' He sounded embarrassed, as if what he was about to say sounded preposterous even to his ears. 'He says your visitor threatened him with a gun.' Ella laughed, the man's laughter joining hers. 'I know, I know, but I do have to check it out, and he's got a black eye.'

'Brian, I haven't had any visitors and as it happens, I'm packing. I've decided to leave and come back next year.'

'Oh.' He sounded disappointed. 'Mind you, I can understand. It's not been an easy time for you.'

'No, it hasn't, and you can tell the dean that it hasn't been made any easier by people like Al Brown harassing me and pulling stupid pranks like this.'

'I see. I didn't realize but I will certainly mention it to the dean. Now, you will come and have a chat before you go?'

'Of course. I'll see you later.' She closed the door but held her finger up to her lips and waited. A moment or two later she relaxed and smiled but was still quiet as she said, 'Porter—nice enough. You don't know anything about hitting somebody, threatening him with a gun?'

Lucas shrugged and said, 'I'm not used to people being rude to me.'

'Don't worry—most people around here would vote to give you an honorary degree, a doctorate if you'd killed him.' She laughed and sat back on the edge of the bed.

'What about my question?'

'The answer's obvious, isn't it? I don't really want him in prison: I want him dead. I want him to suffer. And what you're really asking me is whether I wanna head down that road. Well, I'm not sure I do, but what's the alternative?'

'Get on with your life. Not here, maybe, but somewhere.'

She shook her head slowly and said, 'I can't. It's eating away at me. Sometimes it even makes me feel sick, like I need to throw up. I just know I'll never rest until I find Ben's killers. I can't.' It could have been a slip but equally, he could imagine how her focus had narrowed to avenging her brother's death, a death she'd probably never made provision for.

'Okay. Where are you going?'

'I've booked into the Savoy.' She laughed, he supposed at her own extravagance. 'It's just until I sort out somewhere permanent. I want to get settled in there before telling Simon. He'll want me to go back to his place otherwise, and I need to look after myself.'

'Give me your mobile number.' She looked shocked by his abruptness, but wrote it down on a piece of paper. 'I'll be in touch as soon as I know something. In the meantime, you can still call me on the usual number.'

'How long do you think it might be, before you're in touch?'

'It could be soon. The Savoy's a nice place. Relax, look for a house. I'll call.'

'Okay. And thanks.'

'Did you tell the police about me?'

For a second she looked baffled by the question but said, 'No. I mean, yes, that you existed, but we agreed to say we didn't know your name or where your house was.' He was relieved.

'That's good. One more question. I need to ask Chris a few things, just about what he might have seen, stuff like that. What room is he in?'

As if breaking bad news, she said, 'Chris and I aren't seeing each other anymore.'

'I gathered. I still need to talk to him.'

'Langford, B15. I can show you where it is.'

'I'll find it.' He stood up and said, 'Take care. I'll be in touch.'

It was only as he was walking back across the quad that he thought of all the things he should have said—that he was sorry she and Chris had broken up, that he wanted to be there for her, that she was a good person and deserved better than this. She also deserved better than him, and her willingness to subject herself to the awkwardness of his company said something about how desperate she was.

Langford was a more relaxed, more open place. A couple of people said hi to him as he walked along the corridor and most of the doors were open, the mix of music melding in the corridor into some kind of progressive jazz rock.

Chris's door was open. He was sitting at his desk working. Lucas stepped into the room a little and knocked. Chris looked up and jumped nervously before regaining his composure.

'Can I come in?'

'Jesus! Uh, yeah, sure.' He gestured him in and Lucas sat on the edge of the bed.

'I need to ask you something and I need the truth. Did you tell the police about me?'

Before he could say anything else, Chris turned contrite and said, 'I'm sorry, I didn't want to, but they kept saying, "You're sure you didn't hear his name?" And you didn't tell us we had to keep it secret, just that it would be better.'

'I know. It's not a problem.' If anything, he was pleased because it had been Chris; if someone else had given his identity to the police it might have been something to worry about.

'It didn't make things difficult for you?'

He shrugged and said, 'I had a courtesy call, but it's not in their interest to come after someone like me. You've probably made things worse for Ella, though.' Chris looked confused. 'Think about it. She stuck with what you agreed, so the police probably think she's a liar, that she knows more than she's saying about everything.'

'Yeah. Look, I'm sorry about that . . .' He stopped himself and said, 'Are you working for her? Is that why you're here?'

'I'm helping her through a tough time, that's all.'

Chris shifted in his seat, his voice finding a higher pitch. 'Look, it's easy to think I've been a bastard here but, Jesus, we were only going out. There's married couples would split up after something like that happened to them. And I'm twenty. I'm too young to get tied into a relationship that intense.'

'I agree.'

He was surprised, and his voice was more relaxed when he finally said, 'That's not the only reason I bailed, though. I mean, it's easy to think I'm the cold one but she's freezing up inside. I tried to get through to her over the summer, I really did, but she turned her back on me first. She's become so obsessed with finding the culprits, she's losing sight of what's around her, other people.'

Lucas mused for a second over his use of the word *culprits*, a strangely innocent-sounding word for the people he was talking about. Then he said, 'I don't see it, but even if it's true, don't you think it's understandable?'

'Maybe. Look, I'm sorry, call me shallow, but my life doesn't have to be that complicated, not yet. Ella's a great person, and I'm really sorry this happened to her, but it happened to her, not us, not me. What can I say? I hope she gets her life back.' Lucas sensed that maybe he was meant to say something in response but wasn't sure what. After a pause, Chris filled the gap himself, saying, 'You have any idea who did it?'

Lucas shrugged nonchalantly and said, 'Not yet. But a hit like this shouldn't be too hard to trace.' Chris nodded but looked like there was something he needed to get off his chest, something he was nervous about sharing.

'You think it's the uncle.'

Chris looked shocked. 'How did you know?'

'Wild guess.'

'I don't have any real reason to think it's him. It was just, when I met him in the summer . . . I don't know. He seemed phony, like someone covering up.'

'You could be right. I'll kill him.'

'Jesus, no, I only . . .' Lucas smiled and he sputtered to a stop. 'You have the weirdest sense of humor I've ever encountered.'

'You're still young.' Lucas stood to leave and said, 'Nice meeting you. Good luck.' He hesitated as he walked towards the door, drawn to an array of photos on the wall. Ella was in quite a few of them but no more prominent than a number of other repeated faces, a bunch of kids messing around, doing stupid stuff, at the beach, skiing.

'Will I see you again at all?'

Lucas turned, trying to work out whether he was nervous or hopeful, and said, 'Wouldn't imagine so.' There was the answer; Chris was relieved.

And in a strange way, he was hurt by that, because he'd liked Chris. He'd have happily killed him for blowing their cover in

Florence but he'd truly liked him, even envied him. He'd turned his back on Ella, an act of weakness that wasn't a million miles from the one Lucas had performed fifteen years before with Madeleine, but apart from that he was the kind of kid he would have liked to have been himself.

He hadn't been that kid, though, and if her life hadn't been destroyed Ella Hatto would never have needed him. But here he was, preparing to guide her through the wreckage to the dark core of her family. Chris was probably right about who they'd find there, too.

Lucas had thought about suggesting it to her himself. For all he knew she was still in danger. Worse still, she could force her uncle's hand if she let him know what she was doing. He'd said nothing, though, aware of the emotional impact it would have on her, aware too that they could be wrong.

And something told him that she wouldn't tell her uncle. She was probably in denial, refusing to believe that the man who'd taken her in had also tried to kill her, but somewhere deep within her she had to suspect him, a suspicion that would keep her cautious. Maybe that was the real reason she'd checked into a hotel. She knew. Deep down, she had to know, and he was confident that she wouldn't put herself in danger, that she'd be vigilant.

He was confident too that if the trail did lead to her uncle, her need for vengeance would be all the greater for having denied it, her wrath intensified by the acts of kindness he'd shown her in the past three months. If Simon Hatto was behind it, no amount of smiles and sympathy would help him now; his only hope was to do what he should have done in the first place, and finish the job he'd started.

Chapter Twelve

The guy at reception was polite, obsequious even, but in a way that managed to be cold and vaguely condescending. It was clear too that Lucas didn't look at all familiar to him, even though he'd stayed in the hotel for a couple of nights just over a week ago.

He'd almost finished checking in when something stirred in the receptionist's memory and he picked up a note from behind the desk, saying, 'Oh, Mr. Lucas, there's a gentleman waiting in the bar for you.'

'What kind of gentleman?'

'Young, Australian, wearing a suit.' The final words somehow managed to convey a disapproval of Lucas's casual dress. 'The bar's just through there.'

'I know. I've stayed here before.'

'Of course.'

He walked through to the bar, where Dan was sitting on a stool, deep in conversation with the barman. When he saw Lucas, he stood up, smiling as they shook hands.

'Good journey?'

Lucas nodded.

'How about a drink? They've got an eighteen-year-old Macallan.'

'Sure.'

'I'll have one too. Rico?' The barman nodded and the two of them sat down at a table, Dan saying, 'Rico's from Brazil, shoe designer for catwalk shows.' Lucas laughed to himself, that Dan had been there maybe twenty minutes and already knew the barman's name and story. The next time he went in there he'd probably get his drinks on the house.

'So, Novakovic.'

'Yeah, Novakovic,' said Dan, repeating the name like it was a toast. 'How'd you get the lead on him anyway?'

'I called in on Lo Bello, asked him who might do a job like that in London.'

'He mention me?'

Lucas smiled, amused by Dan's vanity. 'In passing. We both concluded this was probably a bit low-rent for you.'

Dan laughed, 'I can't believe you actually know Lo Bello— that's so cool.'

'I used to know everyone.' He wanted to add something about it all being a long time ago but held his tongue, saying instead, 'So where is our friend Novakovic?'

'Under our noses. West London, room in a house with a load of other Balkan boys, most of them illegals. Could be unpredictable, so I was thinking I'd pick you up around four this morning, get in there while they're all in bed.'

'Sounds good.'

The waiter put their drinks down.

'Thanks, Rico.' Dan picked up his glass and said, 'Good health, and good to have you back in the game, mate.'

Lucas raised his glass too but said, 'I'm not back in the game.'

Dan smiled, disbelieving, but became distracted by the honey-eyed scent of the whisky in his glass. And why should Dan believe him? Lucas was here and he'd killed people that summer and had implicitly agreed to kill another. The only extent to which he wasn't back in the game was his own fragile conviction that he'd finished with it.

'So what have you been up to?'

'Not much. I run in the summer, ski in the winter. I read, I think.'

'Dangerous,' said Dan. He looked intrigued. 'Don't you miss it, though? I mean, what happened in Italy—didn't it give you that buzz again?'

'A little.' He thought back but there was no adrenaline in the memory of it, only the torment of Ella Hatto and the strangely intertwined thoughts of Paris and Madeleine and Isabelle. 'I saw my daughter this summer.'

Dan put his drink down, shocked, saying, 'Jesus! I didn't know you'd been married, but a daughter!'

'We weren't married, and when I say I saw my daughter, I don't mean I met her. I just saw her.' He smiled, thinking of her sitting in that cafe. 'But no kidding, Dan, it gave me more of a buzz than anything I've done in the last twenty years.'

Dan nodded. 'I bet.' He seemed deep in thought for a while, then, 'You know, this business tonight, I can handle it on my own if you want.'

'No, this job's personal; I want to see it through.' He knew that was a lie, though, and that if Madeleine had reacted any differently he probably wouldn't have been there.

Dan picked him up at four and they drove out of central London, passing a steady flow of light traffic until they got out into the scruffy western no-man's-land where rows of old houses were divided into bed-sits and individual rooms, crammed with immigrants and asylum-seekers, the underside of the melting-pot.

As Dan parked, he said, 'Our man's in the middle room on the ground floor.'

'Makes life easier.' Lucas attached his silencer and added, 'Remember, though, I don't want anyone getting hurt.'

'Are we included in that?' He smiled and got out of the car.

There was a mattress in the small front yard and the smell of rotting food. The house looked like it needed some work, even in the forgiving glow of the streetlights. He'd done business over the years with the people-smuggling rackets and he couldn't believe this was what the immigrants were all so desperate to reach.

Neither of the doors posed a problem and the house remained darkly silent and stifled as they moved swiftly from the street door and into the bedroom. Dan turned the light on, but Novakovic came around only as Lucas put the gun to his head, and even then, managed little more than a drowsy downbeat acknowledgment.

Dan threw off the duvet and gestured for him to sit up. Lucas backed away slightly with the gun and Novakovic sat up, naked, sinewy and powerful. But when Dan asked him quietly where his gun was he pointed languidly at a chest of drawers.

Dan dug around in the top drawer and took out a couple of guns. Lucas glanced around the rest of the room, surprisingly tidy given there was so much crammed into it. It was bare of any personality, though; no books, posters, nothing to hint at the kind of person he might be.

And considering he was developing something of a reputation, Lucas had to wonder what kind of fee he commanded. After all, he'd been called in to do a job like the Hattos and yet here he was living in one cramped room in a slum of a house. It made him pity the guy, whatever his motivation.

'Okay, let him get dressed. I'll keep a watch at the door.' Lucas stepped out into the hall, closing the bedroom door behind him.

He walked the few paces to the kitchen, making sure it was empty, then back to the door, listening carefully to the occasional sounds from the rest of the house: someone shifting about in bed, floorboards creaking, a cough, light snoring.

Then the commotion started, as violent and immediate against that background as gunfire itself. Novakovic was shouting in Serbo-Croatian like he was trying to alert the other people in the house. Lucas heard Dan hit him and the screaming stopped as Novakovic fell heavily against a chair or table. Then a moment later it started again as more furniture bounced around the room.

Lucas strained to hear the rest of the house above the struggle. There was definitely movement, and that was the last thing he wanted. The door of the next room opened and a bleary head looked out, retreating as soon as he saw Lucas. Maybe they were used to being raided by police or immigration and knew when to keep out of the way.

The din continued, though, and the bleary-headed guy came running out again, waving what looked like a knife, his figure silhouetted against the light behind him. Lucas wasn't sure it was a knife, but he shot him anyway. The guy dropped a couple of feet short of where he was standing.

There was panicked shouting upstairs now, then a gunshot, a startling crack that silenced the voices and momentarily silenced Novakovic before he resumed, shriller, louder.

Like a delayed response to the gunshot, a body tumbled down the stairs. The hallway and landing lights came on almost as he hit the bottom and then the second voice above resumed on its own, angry and desperate, wailing with the realization of what he'd just done.

Lucas looked at the two bodies, both young Eastern Europeans. The first had been holding a bread knife and was in his underwear. The second was wearing jeans and had a wound on his neck that was still gently pumping blood, his eyes startled.

Another shot cracked out, hitting the wall near the bottom of the street door, then another, before the guy with the gun hurtled down the stairs, screaming in fury, firing again. Lucas fired a shot up through the stair railings and the guy stumbled, his momentum vaulting him over the body at the bottom of the stairs and leaving him splayed awkwardly on the floor beyond.

He was dead—another young guy, lean and pale and red-haired, wearing track-suit bottoms. It was quiet in the house now, even in the room behind him. Lucas took a step towards the latest body, curious. He spotted the wound then, a lucky hit, up into the side of his abdomen, the bullet probably bouncing around inside his rib cage before lodging.

If there was anyone else in the house, they'd clearly decided on keeping quiet and out of the way. Lucas walked back to his position and then a moment later the door opened and Dan was standing there with Novakovic. Novakovic was dressed and cuffed, his face and T-shirt bloody and bruised.

Dan, on the other hand, looked like he'd been out for a stroll—not a hair out of place, his whole demeanor as relaxed and easygoing as it always was.

Lucas smiled and said, 'Problem?'

'Couldn't find his shoes, that's all.' He looked around the hall then and said, 'Jesus H!'

'I only killed two of them.' They both looked at Novakovic but he was taking in the scene coldly, like he'd seen this kind of thing too often to offer up any sadness for it.

They stepped over the bodies and walked back to the car with Novakovic between them. The street was quiet; no bedroom lights, no indication of curiosity about the gunshots that had burst out a minute before. Lucas sat in the back with Novakovic and they drove away, the sky showing the first uncertain hints of daylight.

Dan dropped him along the street from the hotel and said, 'I'll take him back to my place, give him some breakfast, then I'll take him somewhere out of the way.'

'Okay.' Lucas thought about telling him to be careful but it was hardly necessary, and Novakovic was beaten, his spirit so visibly broken now that Lucas had to wonder how he'd got this far without being taken down. He looked like someone who'd been waiting these last seven years for his own history to catch up with him, whatever it was he'd temporarily escaped from back there in Bosnia.

Lucas slept for a couple of hours, then ordered breakfast and watched the news channel. He was waiting to see something of what had gone on but there was nothing, either because it still hadn't been reported or because no one thought it mattered that much.

Novakovic wouldn't matter that much either, except to Ella. She'd want him dead, but Lucas would try to steer her away from that course. It wasn't that he wanted to spare Novakovic's life, but that he thought he could protect Ella from the ugliness of what lay ahead of her.

And for all he knew, she didn't want to be protected from it. Lucas couldn't be sure what she wanted, or how far she'd strayed from the girl she'd been three months before, but he had an idea that the fate of Novakovic might tell him.

Chapter Thirteen

Simon saw her first. She'd been surveying the bar from the top of the steps for thirty seconds or more before she noticed him waving in exaggerated slow motion. She laughed and walked over to him, kissed him on the cheek.

As they sat down, he said, 'Well I can see why you chose this over coming and staying with us again.'

She looked around and said, 'It's basic, I know, but it'll do until I find somewhere permanent.' The waiter came over. 'I'll have a Pussyfoot, please. Simon?'

'Oh, just a Coke or a mineral water or something.'

'Make that two Pussyfoots.' The waiter smiled and left. 'Fuddy-duddy!'

'I'm sorry it didn't work out for you back at college. You know if there's anything I can do . . .'

She appreciated the offer but knew that Simon couldn't help her with the one thing she really wanted.

'Thanks. And you know, I didn't come here because I was unhappy with you and Lucy. I just thought it was time to pick up the pieces, become a bit more independent.'

He nodded his understanding and said, 'Do you plan to go back at all? To college?'

'Next year, perhaps. I'll see how I feel nearer the time.' The waiter put some snacks on their table. She picked an almond out. 'I suppose life just suddenly feels too serious to be at college.'

'Perhaps it'll feel different next year.' The drinks arrived and Simon looked slightly embarrassed by the extravagance of the glass and its contents.

She laughed and said, 'It's nonalcoholic. Try it.'

He sucked on his straw and admitted defeat. 'Yes, it's pretty good.' He still seemed vaguely uncomfortable, as if the drink's appearance was out of step with his image of himself. 'Now, I don't think it's a good idea for you to do nothing with your time so I've put together some homework for you.' He looked around, then reached down and took a folder out of a briefcase next to his chair. She'd never seen him or her father carrying a briefcase before and it looked out of place. She wondered if it was his or if he'd borrowed it. 'These are some profiles of the various companies within the family business. If you feel like visiting any of them, seeing how they operate, it's easy to arrange.'

'All in good time, perhaps. I am interested and I will look through this but . . .'

'I know. I understand. You don't have to get involved. But it's good for you to know a bit more about it, just in case.'

She finished the sentence in her head, knowing that he meant just in case he wasn't around, and she said, 'You don't think we're still in danger?'

'No!' He was almost too dismissive.

'But we could be. I mean, why did they try so hard to kill me and then just give up? And the police—they don't *know* we're safe. They removed the protection because nothing happened over the summer, but that doesn't mean anything.' Too much had spilled out, giving the impression she'd been dwelling on these things, which she had.

Simon looked calm, though, as he said, 'This is why I want you to put your mind to something else. Look at the file.' She put the folder next to her on the banquette and patted it.

Her phone rang then and she looked at the call display. 'Estate agent,' she said to Simon as she answered it. 'Hello?'

'Are you still in the Savoy?'

She felt visibly flustered for a second but Simon was poking noncommittally at the snacks. 'Oh, hi, Peter. Yes, I'm in the American Bar with my uncle at the moment.'

'Can you be ready in half an hour?'

'Half an hour?' She looked at Simon and he gestured for her to go ahead. 'Yeah, that should be fine.'

'I'll pick you up.'

'Okay. See you then.' She hung up the phone and said, 'It's a flat in Kensington. They've been really awkward about viewing so I didn't want to pass up on it.'

'Don't worry about it. I have to dash off soon anyway.' He took one more mouthful of his drink, picked up his briefcase.

'Simon, I don't mean to go on, but don't you ever wonder if they're still out there? I mean, don't you ever wonder if they're just biding their time, if they'll have another go at us?'

He frowned slightly. 'Sometimes. Luce worries about it, as you can imagine. She still checks on the boys two or three times in the night. But I think whoever wanted Mark dead must feel avenged enough by now, and must be smart enough to know that killing you or me won't add anything to that revenge.'

'You don't think about getting revenge yourself?'

'Of course,' he said, a touch of sadness in his face. 'Irony is, Mark probably would have known people who could take it for him. But we don't. All we have is the police, for what it's worth. No good thinking about revenge—all the things they say about it are true.'

She nodded and felt guilty for keeping Lucas a secret from him. She knew all the clichés about revenge, too—how it served no purpose and provided no gain. But she was locked onto this path because she needed to know who'd killed them, and once she knew, how could she not want them to suffer for what they'd done?

She'd thought she wanted justice, but Lucas had opened her eyes to that paper-thin fallacy. Justice, even if it were done, would mean a prison sentence and that would never be enough. The burden of the survivor was hers; that's all there was to it. They had to die.

When Lucas picked her up, she was in the car for a minute or so before she realized it was his Mercedes from Switzerland.

'You drove here? I mean, to England?'

'It's not a bad trip, and I had to call on a couple of people en route.'

She took in the surroundings, feeling oddly connected to his world again by being there. She opened the glove compartment where the CDs were but instead of the previous selection there was a new series of discs.

'You're learning French?'

'Trying to. *C'est très difficile.*'

She was puzzled by this apparent branching out; he didn't strike her as someone who liked stepping outside his routine. She was about to press him on the subject but he said, 'Aren't you curious as to why I called you or where we're going?'

'I just assumed you found out something.'

'I found the guy who killed your family. I'm taking you to him.'

'Already?' She couldn't believe it. After a summer of inertia and frustration she hadn't expected Lucas to produce results in a little over a week. She wasn't even certain she was ready.

'This was the easy bit. I haven't found the guy who ordered the hits. I've found the guy who carried them out. But he'll lead us to someone else and so on.'

She wanted to tell him to turn back to the hotel, to hand the man over to the police and let them follow his leads, to forget about the whole thing. And yet she wanted to see him, to see the last face her brother had seen as he'd looked up from his bed. She wanted to look into those eyes and see what was there.

'Where is he?'

'In a derelict engine shed. Wouldn't have been my choice but the guy I have working for me has a melodramatic streak.'

'You're holding him captive?'

'I don't think he'd have accepted an invite.'

'Did he put up a fight?'

'No, it was . . . We just brought him in. He's a Bosnian Serb, Vasko Novakovic, based in London for about seven years, works for himself.'

'Has he told you anything?'

'I haven't spoken to him yet.'

'Will he tell us anything?'

'Who can say?' He paused and she expected it to go on indefinitely, but after a few seconds he added, 'I was wrong, by the way. As far as anyone knows, your dad didn't have any enemies.'

'But . . .'

'I mean from the old days. Whoever did this is probably someone close to him now, a disgruntled employee, or . . . Well, someone close, anyway.'

She found it hard to believe that anyone who'd known her father or worked for him could have hated him that much. A business rival, yes, or someone he'd inadvertently crossed in the past, but not someone close; her dad hadn't been the kind of person to inspire that kind of hatred. It had to be a stranger, just like the stranger Lucas was driving her to now.

'I think you're wrong. I mean, surely you can't account for everyone from the past, and you can't account for business rivals. Think of all the businesses he owned.' She thought of the folder Simon had given her and decided to study it when she got back to the hotel. 'I just can't see it being an employee.'

'Maybe not.'

He fell silent. He seemed to be enjoying part of this, the intrigue perhaps. She hadn't thought so in Italy but maybe he enjoyed the killing too, finding some thrill in pulling the trigger and ending a life. For all she knew, the man he was taking her to was the same. Perhaps rather than doing the job coldly and dispassionately he'd knocked on the door of their family home and got a power trip out of the murders he'd committed there—a seductive combination of pleasure and profit all rolled up into the destruction of a family.

They drove across a stretch of wasteland before reaching the brick engine shed, its windows smashed, part of the roof missing. Buddleia bushes were growing wild around it, still full of purple flowers but looking forlorn in these surroundings.

Lucas parked alongside the shed next to a Range Rover and they got out of the car. A train ran past on one of the lines about fifty yards away with a short, half-hearted roar before dying away. She wondered how many of the people on board had noticed them there. It made her conscious that she'd left the law behind, that she was becoming the person the police had half suspected her of being.

She followed Lucas into the shed. With part of the roof missing it was bright inside and weeds and a single buddleia were growing among the debris and broken glass. It had the oily smell of industry and decay about it.

As soon as she walked in, she noticed the guy standing in the middle of the shed: short dark hair, lean, wearing a black suit with a black shirt underneath. It took her a moment longer to see the other man sitting on the floor, his arms handcuffed behind his back. He looked broken and dejected, his hair disheveled, face bruised, T-shirt dirty and bloodstained. And he looked young. Lucas had talked about him being in London for seven years and she'd imagined someone older, not a guy in his mid-twenties.

'Ella, this is Dan Borowski. Dan, Ella.' The guy in the black suit smiled at her. He was in his mid to late twenties too, and good-looking, but she was unnerved because he looked so much like the stereotype of what she supposed he was—a contract killer or a gangster, somebody from the underworld. 'And this is Vasko Novakovic.' Lucas turned back to Dan and said, 'Thanks. I'll call you later.'

'No worries.' Dan looked down at Novakovic and then at Lucas again. 'He's heard of me but he hasn't heard of you. How about that?' Lucas nodded at Dan, amused. Dan left and she heard his Range Rover pull away across the gravel, then another train passing.

'Come over. Take a closer look at him.' She stepped closer. Novakovic looked up at her and away again. 'We don't want to hurt you. All we need is information.' He looked up at Lucas, disbelieving. 'Mark Hatto, his wife, his son. Where did the hit come from?'

He nodded, a grim acknowledgment, as if he'd known that job would lead him into trouble. He seemed to weigh things before shrugging and saying, 'Bruno Brodsky.' Lucas smiled at Ella, a look of self-satisfaction, though she had no idea why.

'Ask him why he killed my brother.'

Novakovic looked at her in surprise, as if realizing for the first time how she was involved. 'He doesn't have to ask me. My English is good.' He hesitated before saying, 'I was paid for three people—your father, mother, brother.'

'He was only seventeen,' said Ella.

Novakovic looked unimpressed. 'I do what I'm paid to do. Brodsky tells me kill the boy, I kill the boy. Brodsky tells me kill you, I kill you.'

He seemed almost to be gloating and she could feel her confused and overwhelmed emotions settle into disgust and hatred. When she'd first seen him sitting there, she'd hoped he might be full of remorse, that she might even be able to find a way to forgive him.

But he didn't care anything for what he'd done to her or her family. If anything, he seemed to be reveling in it. She felt sick, too, because she knew that even when Lucas killed him it wouldn't erase the memory of that smug arrogance.

'Okay, Ella, let's go.' They both looked at Lucas in surprise and he said, 'He was the messenger, not the murderer. It's difficult, but you need to see that distinction—there's no revenge here.'

It took her a moment or two to soak up the absurdity of this. She thought of her mum and dad, of Ben lying perfect and lost in that casket, and she knew in every cell of her being that she wanted this monster dead, as ultimately unsatisfying as she knew that would be.

'Kill him.'

'What are you going to do, Ella—kill everyone who came anywhere near this contract?'

'Just him. Lucas, I'll pay you, but how can I let him live knowing what he did? How can I?' He didn't respond. 'You're saying it was just a job for him. Well, make it just a job for you. I'll pay you whatever the going rate is but you have to kill him. You have to.'

'I told you before, no payments.' She didn't even see him draw his gun, just heard the sudden ear-cracking of the shot, a sound so violent it startled her. When she recovered, she looked at Novakovic. He was lying on his back, his body contorted and in tight relief against his T-shirt, forced that way by the obstacle of his own arms handcuffed behind him. It reminded her of one of those Michelangelo statues they'd seen in Italy, a dying slave— except for his face, mashed with blood, stripped of form, no longer looking human.

She felt more satisfied than she'd expected, having erased the only extant memory of her family's final moments and death. And she knew also now that the struggle she'd been having between the desires for justice and revenge had been a false one.

This had been both. In her mind, she wanted justice for her family but in her gut she wanted revenge, and both were measured on the same scale, achievable by the same means. And though she'd finally broken the law, she knew she'd done right.

Novakovic was dead but she felt an uncontrollable urge now to hit him, to spit on him, or to do what Lucas had done, to fire a bullet into him. A part of her wanted to feel what it was like, but more than that, she wanted in some small way to claim this first act of revenge for herself. She felt a mix of shame and excitement at the thought of it, but she wanted his blood on her hands.

Lucas was still holding the gun at his side. She held out her hand and said, 'Do you mind?'

He seemed puzzled and glanced at the body as if to make sure he was dead. Then he gave her the gun. Holding it in both hands, she aimed at the bloody mess of Novakovic's head. She closed her eyes as she started to squeeze the trigger, but forced herself to open them again.

The noise and force of the shot still came as a shock, and she didn't see if she'd hit him. His face didn't look any different so she turned to Lucas and said, 'Did I hit him?' He nodded and reached out to take the gun from her. 'Thanks. I'm sure it seems sick but . . .' She felt weak suddenly, like a blood-sugar dive, ambushed in mid-sentence by a shakiness and a swell of emotion. She tried to rally herself, not wanting Lucas to think it had anything to do with seeing Novakovic killed. 'I had to.' That was all her voice would allow.

'Sure.' He put the gun away and walked out. Once they were sitting in the car, he said, 'Don't ever ask me to do that for you again.'

She wasn't sure why he was unhappy with her. 'I thought that's what we came here for. And I didn't ask you to do it for me. I asked you to do it for my family.'

'I appreciate that, but don't ask me again. I'm finished with killing people.' He started the car and pulled away.

'But what about when we find the person who . . .'

'I'll make an exception, but only the one. This is revenge, not therapy. You need to work something out of your system, join a gym.'

'Sorry.' She wasn't sure why she was apologizing, except that she felt chastened, uncomfortable with the thought that she might have earned his disapproval. She didn't know what he expected of her, but she was disappointed that she'd fallen short in some way.

Trying to move the conversation on, she said, 'You were pleased when he told you who'd sent him.'

'Bruno Brodsky. He's a fixer, based in Budapest. Some of these people can be slippery but I've known Bruno a long time; he'll tell us what he knows.'

'So we're going to Budapest?'

'There's no need for you to go. I thought you'd want to see the killer.' He laughed. 'And boy, did you want to see him. But there's no reason for you to see Bruno.'

'I want to. I mean, I'll only sit here wondering otherwise. And I wanna hear what he's got to say because I wanna understand. I need to know everything.'

'Okay. There's no reason you shouldn't come if you want to. I'm warning you, though, don't even think of asking me to kill Brodsky. He's a middleman, that's all, and he's going to help us find who ordered the hit. You have to respect that.'

'I will.'

They were back on the road now and she relaxed into her seat. She was strangely content, fulfilled. They were getting somewhere. Lucas seemed to be having doubts, maybe out of some desire to shield her. She was certain he'd come around, though. He had to, because she was determined these people would pay for what they'd done, all of them, and she could see no reason to make an exception for Bruno Brodsky or anybody else.

Chapter Fourteen

Lucas sat in the limousine. Ella's flight from London had landed so he didn't expect her to be long. He'd considered going to see Bruno before Ella arrived but had stopped himself. The way she'd acted with Novakovic had thrown him but that was no reason to start cutting her out of the loop.

He'd tried to imagine himself in her position. She'd led a sheltered life, only to see her security violated, so maybe she deserved a little hunger for revenge. And it had been born out of love, a love for her parents and brother that he couldn't begin to comprehend.

He could think of only two people in the world he'd be that desperate to avenge and yet one of them couldn't bear to look at him and the other barely knew he existed. That didn't leave him in much of a position to judge Ella for her bitterness.

The door opened and she got into the back seat next to him, smiling, saying hello, a few words about the flight. She was wearing a vaguely oriental-looking trouser suit, still casual but smarter than he was used to seeing her.

They chatted on their way into Budapest, about her flight, about the city, but all she wanted was to see Bruno. When they got to the hotel, she said, 'I'll just take a quick shower and get rid of my bags. Half an hour?'

'Sure. I'll wait here.'

The lobby was modern and spacious. He took a seat on the far side, next to two portholes in the wall that looked in on a large aquarium with a reef and tropical fish. For a while, he looked out at the businessmen and well-heeled tourists who occupied a handful of the other tables in the lobby. When he tired of looking at them, he turned to the coral reef behind the two portholes.

He'd been staring at it for a few minutes, studying the movements of the fish, before he realized it wasn't one large aquarium but two separate tanks next to each other, the sides of each mirrored to produce an appearance of continuity.

Right now a large silver fish with yellow fins was looking at its own reflection, mesmerized. It was the only one of its kind in the tank but there was another in the neighboring tank, an isolation that seemed profoundly cruel.

None of these fish, no matter how sentient they might be, could have any concept of the other tank's existence, let alone the existence of tropical oceans far away. It disturbed him, and then it disturbed him more to look around the lobby and see all these people, none of whom had even noticed it.

He'd read enough books to know why it troubled him, to recognize it as a metaphor for his own life, life in general. That made it no less disturbing, though, no less full of truth. He was left feeling restless and full of urgency, as if he'd suddenly realized that he didn't have enough time, that with every passing minute it was becoming too late.

Yet here he was, being pulled back into the world he'd supposedly rejected, sitting in a hotel lobby in Budapest, waiting to meet Bruno Brodsky. It was like he'd thrown away the last four years, justifying Madeleine's rejection of him in the process.

Ella had changed when she came back down. It took him a second to recognize the sarong-style skirt, the one they'd bought in Florence, the one she'd worn on the journey to Switzerland. He'd been vaguely attracted to her back then. Now he found her almost like someone with a scent of illness about her. 'It's a nice day; I thought we'd walk to Bruno's.'

'Sounds good. I could do with the walk.' She looked over at the portholes and for a moment he thought she'd say something about them, but she looked away blankly. That was the point, he supposed—that people weren't meant to show an interest, merely to register them as part of the relaxing ambiance. It made him want to shoot the place up.

It was a nice walk to Bruno's, the city warm, full of light, lively. It was looking good too—moneyed, the way it always should have been. Ella seemed impressed, drinking it all in like a tourist, pointing things out to him, a glimpse of the Ella he'd encountered at the beginning of the summer, the girl who'd been lost somewhere in the intervening grief.

At one point she said, 'Chris and I were gonna come here this summer.'

'I know.'

'Of course.' She laughed and said, 'If you'd told me then that this is how I'd finally visit Budapest! Kind of like *To the Lighthouse*.'

He nodded and said, 'Virginia Woolf—boy, am I glad she's dead.' Ella laughed again. He liked to see her laugh. 'It's just along here.'

'Oh, right.' As he pressed the buzzer for Bruno's apartment, she said, 'Do you know for sure that he's here? Perhaps he's away.'

Lucas kept listening for a pickup at the other end but shook his head and said, 'As far as I know he hasn't been out of the city in twenty-five years; that's when his wife died. He visits her grave every morning, without fail.'

'So he's quite old?'

147

Lucas took a moment to work out where she was coming from before saying, 'No, no, she died when they were both really young—he's only about fifty now.'

She nodded towards the intercom and said, 'Doesn't look like he's in, though.'

'No.'

'How did she die?'

'I don't know. I never asked.' He looked around, wondering which of his haunts to try first, spurred finally by the feel of the sun on his face. 'Terrace of the cafe at the Gellert—that's where he'll be on a day like today.'

He started walking and she said, 'You seem to know him pretty well.'

'I know his routine.' He couldn't be sure of that anymore, though, and was beginning to think he should have done some checking before coming out here, to feel nervous of looking amateurish and out of touch.

They picked up a taxi and as soon as they got out at the Gellert, he knew he should never have doubted himself. He could already see Bruno sitting on the terrace to the left of the main entrance, talking away into his phone, doing business.

He looked like he'd lost some weight but he was still a big guy, wide and heavy-boned. His hair was thinning too but still so black it looked like it had been dyed. He looked pretty healthy, tanned, relaxed as he chatted away.

He kept talking as they approached but glanced up and then seized, muttering something into the phone before ending the call. Lucas knew what he was thinking and was impressed by how calm he looked under the circumstances.

He didn't say anything until Lucas had reached the table and then simply, 'Is this it?' It almost made Lucas feel nostalgic for the past, for the power he'd had over people's lives.

'No. How are you, Bruno?' Only now did his nervousness show, his hand shaking as he reached for his iced tea, a twitching smile struggling to take control of his face. A waitress walked over as they sat down and Lucas said, 'Iced tea for me, please.'

'Make that two,' said Ella.

Bruno finally laughed and said, 'I wish you'd called first.'

'I don't think that would have been a wise move. Do you?'

'Potentially not. I'm hearing nothing about you for over two years and then the grapevine is telling me you're the one who interferes with one of my jobs in Italy. Three good people.'

'They weren't that good.'

Bruno shrugged and said, 'Could be so. Two Albanians. The young Italian, he could have shown some promise. But I expected a bodyguard, not a Lucas.'

He felt a slight twinge of unease because the young Italian really had shown some promise, slipping undetected beneath his radar. But it was buried by something more significant: the fact that Bruno had expected a bodyguard.

'You knew she'd have a bodyguard?'

Bruno looked confused for a second and said, 'Not before the job started, but obviously, somebody took the two Albanians down—I didn't think it was a member of the public.'

'Oh.' Lucas gestured towards Ella and said, 'This is the job I interfered with.'

Bruno was clearly captivated. 'So you're Ella Hatto. You look different from your pictures. Prettier. It's a pleasure to meet you.' He shook her hand. Ella looked uncomfortable and Lucas realized how inappropriate this whole conversation was. 'Also, I'm sorry about your family.'

'You ordered their murders.' Her voice was forceful, full of indignation.

'I arranged them. That might not seem a distinction to you, but it is. And I am sorry.' The waitress arrived with the drinks, a welcome diversion, and then Bruno lifted his glass and said to Lucas, 'To business.'

'To retirement.'

Bruno laughed and said, 'I don't think so. It's like soldiers—old hitmen never die; they simply disappear.'

'Who killed my family?'

He looked at Ella, acknowledging the interruption with a small nod, and said to both of them, 'That's why you're here?'

'That's why we're here,' said Lucas. 'The calling in of favors.'

'I wasn't aware I owed you any.' He smiled and said, 'It was all done anonymously. Payment came from a numbered account. But you're in luck. I recognized the number, you know, a familiar pattern of digits. So I'm curious to know who this was and I check my records.'

'Who was it?'

Lucas had asked the question but Bruno looked at Ella as he said, 'The contract to kill your family, and you also, came from London, from Larsen Grohl.'

She turned to Lucas. 'Have you heard of him?'

Before he could answer Bruno said, 'Not *him*. Larsen Grohl is a company, corporate security. They've used my services on two previous occasions, not for contracts, just security personnel in the East. For those two occasions, the man who contacted me was named Cooper. This last time, of course, no names.'

Lucas said, 'So it's unusual for this company to take a contract, even for a client?'

'It's my experience. Okay, maybe they're using other people on other occasions but why come to me for this job? No, this is a departure, which I think makes life easier for you.'

'Maybe so,' said Lucas. 'I'll need that bank account number.'

'Call me later, but Lucas, please be quiet about this. If it had been a regular client, you know I wouldn't have given it to you.'

'Sure.' He looked out briefly at the mix of tourists and locals strolling to the thermal baths. There they were with their towels and bags, oblivious—he didn't know whether he envied them or not. 'So long, Bruno.' He shook his hand and got up. Ella seemed surprised, caught mid-gulp. She stood quickly but Bruno remained in his seat and they didn't shake hands.

'If you do come out of retirement, you'll call me first?'

'Better for both of us if I don't.' He hesitated, giving Ella the chance to say something if she wanted to. But she simply walked back toward the waiting taxis and Lucas wondered if she fully appreciated how useful Bruno had been to them.

In the taxi she said, 'Don't believe in hanging around, do you?'

'I did say there was no need for you to come.' It was true, though: he was in a hurry, like he could feel the time running out.

'No, I don't mind. So what now?'

'I'll make some phone calls, find out about Larsen Grohl. We're getting close; it's a big break Bruno's given us.' He could see she was unhappy. And he knew why: because they'd left Bruno happy and healthy on that sunny cafe terrace and she couldn't deal with it. She couldn't understand why they were leaving him unpunished, why they weren't repaying him for the death he'd so efficiently delivered into the Hatto family home. 'What's troubling you?'

She looked out the window at the river, then back to him, hesitating. 'I know he's helped us and I know what you said in London. But surely you understand how it makes me feel to sit and listen to him joking with you about business. Business! Killing people. How can I not hold him responsible?'

'If someone dies in a plane crash you sue the airline, not the travel agent who sold the ticket.'

'You do if the travel agent knew the plane would crash.' Lucas was annoyed with himself for coming up with such a feeble analogy. Maybe she was right anyway; maybe revenge should be merciless and unyielding and he'd been in the business too long to keep sight of that.

He thought of Isabelle, a child he'd given too little thought to during her lifetime. And yet with only the recent locket memories he had of her—walking down the street, sitting in a cafe with friends—he knew that he'd want the same kind of revenge if anything happened to her.

Ella wanted Bruno dead because she'd loved her family and he'd arranged their deaths. Lucas wanted to deflect her from that course, though, for his own selfish reasons, because he didn't want to get dragged back in any further than he had to go.

'All I ask is this. Let's find out who ordered the hit and deal with them first. Avenge your family through them, and after that, if you still feel people like Bruno Brodsky should die too, then so be it.'

She nodded and said, 'Okay, but I want a gun to keep in my room tonight, like before.'

'You don't need a gun,' he said, alarmed by the possibility that she was thinking of doing this on her own.

'How do you know that? For all we know, the contract is still on my head. Brodsky knows I'm in Budapest; he could see it as a chance to clear up unfinished business.'

'I doubt it, but if it makes you happy I'll bring one to your room when we get back.' Still suspicious, he added, 'Did you want to do anything this evening? River cruise, opera, dinner?'

She smiled and said, 'I think I'll just have dinner in my room and have an early night. I've got a few hours before my flight in the morning—I might do some sightseeing then.'

'Sure.' She was lying badly, and it saddened him and left him suspicious that she'd been lying to him since she'd called for his help.

Anger had made her want to see Novakovic dead but he wondered if her urge to shoot him in the head afterwards had been for practice, a premeditated dry run for the acts of revenge she imagined performing.

'Lucas?' He turned to her. She looked defiantly like the innocent he'd first encountered. 'If you'd been paid to kill me, would you have done it?'

'Until four years ago, without even hesitating. Then I became picky, then I got out altogether. Helping your dad was a special favor. So is this.'

He thought she might acknowledge what he'd said, maybe thank him, but she said, 'What happened four years ago?'

He smiled, knowing that it was too insignificant to speak of. He'd been in a department store in Zurich, crowded in the approach to Christmas, and suddenly he'd found a small hand in his. A little girl had reached up to take what she'd thought was her father's hand. The father had seen it happen and had exchanged a little joke in German which Lucas hadn't understood.

That's all it had been, a stupid little incident, the kind of thing that people experienced every day without giving it a thought. But its effect on Lucas had been profound, for reasons transparent enough to be embarrassing. It didn't matter, though, how weakly sentimental the catalyst had been, only that he'd been receptive to it.

'Nothing happened. I just decided to change.' He said no more, and yet he wanted to warn her that it wasn't that easy—something he and Bruno Brodsky and her own father all would have testified to. Once in, there was always a route out; staying out was where the difficulty lay.

But he sensed that she was already too far gone. So instead of giving her advice when they got back to the hotel, he gave her a gun, and a little later still, he called Bruno to get the information he needed and to warn him that Ella was coming.

He waited for her to leave, called Bruno again, ordered some food. Then he set to work making calls, eager to find out what he could about Larsen Grohl, his sense of urgency renewed because he wanted to be done with this before she started drawing attention to him by association.

She was becoming her own creature, and when his old world started to notice her, he didn't want to be there. He'd worked hard at disappearing, too hard for him to throw it all away now by walking into the spotlight with Ella Hatto.

Chapter Fifteen

S he felt sick as she got into the taxi, and guilty too, as if everyone who saw her knew exactly what she was planning to do,
that she had a gun in her bag. The doorman gave the desti-
nation to the driver and he turned and smiled, repeating the words
'*Alkotmany utca*' as if even he knew what she had in mind.

She was scared, but she had to go through with it. Lucas was
like a bureaucrat, so wrapped up in the world he inhabited that he
couldn't see beyond procedure to the truth. It was the done thing
not to touch people like Brodsky because they were facilitators. But
without men like Brodsky, maybe people wouldn't find it so easy to
buy a death. She didn't know that her family would still be alive if
Brodsky hadn't existed, but she knew they were dead because he did.

He'd been told who the targets were—a man, his wife, his
daughter, his seventeen-year-old son—and rather than recoiling in
horror, he'd talked prices. He'd murdered them, his hands no less
bloody than those of Novakovic and whoever it was who'd hated her
father enough to take out the contract.

As the driver turned into the tree-lined street, he said, 'Number?'

'This is fine.' She didn't know the number and anyway, she
didn't want the driver to see where she was going. She waited for

him to pull away before walking up the street, trying to remember in darkness how it had looked during the day.

The first building she stopped at looked familiar but she couldn't find his name on the panel of buzzers. She moved on a couple of buildings until she saw another that looked familiar and this time found what she was looking for.

She opened her bag, double-checking what she knew, that she had the gun, her stomach knotting up on itself at the sight of it. She raised a worryingly shaky hand then and pressed the buzzer. She wasn't sure what she was scared of: killing him or not being able to.

'Hello?'

She stepped closer to the intercom. 'Mr. Brodsky, it's Ella Hatto.'

'Top floor,' he said and buzzed her in. She climbed the first flight of steps, then found the old elevator and took it the rest of the way. He'd left the door ajar for her. She knocked and walked into a small cluttered hallway. 'I'm in here, Ella.'

She walked through the kitchen and into the living room, taking in the high ceilings with their yellow and cream stucco, evidence that this had once been a grand property. On the far side of the room the large windows were open, a breeze blowing through them.

There was a small lamp on in the room and a few large candles burning, the flames being danced close to death by the breeze. Brodsky was sitting to the left of the doorway on one of two modern sofas that filled that corner of the room. A bottle of wine and glasses sat on the coffee table in front of him, a couple of armchairs completing the circle.

She stood behind one of the armchairs and looked at the wine, the two glasses, realizing that he was expecting company. She looked him in the face then. He seemed disappointed. 'So soon? No time for reason?'

At first she didn't understand what he meant, her brain taking a couple of seconds to catch up with itself. She'd taken the gun out as she'd walked through the kitchen and was pointing it at him now. He smiled and looked set to say something else, and she didn't want him to say anything, didn't want to hear reason or have to think of him as a human being.

She lifted the gun and aimed it at the middle of his chest. Conscious that her hands were trembling, she braced herself for the kick and pulled the trigger. Nothing. She pulled it again, getting panicky, all the time staring at his chest, not his face.

'Ella, it isn't loaded.' She heard his words but pulled the trigger again. 'Lucas called me. He told me you'd be coming, that the gun would not be loaded.' She looked at the gun. She couldn't understand. Why would Lucas have betrayed her like that? She backed away, looking around the room for something to defend herself with. Brodsky didn't move, though, and still smiling benevolently, he said, 'Please, come and sit down. I've opened a very nice bottle of red wine. Take a glass with me and tell me why you so want me to die.'

He poured the two glasses of wine. Lucas hadn't betrayed her, just seen through her own betrayal of trust and intervened. He was probably hoping that if she talked to Brodsky, shared a glass of wine with him, she'd begin to see things their way.

'You killed my family.'

'Yes.' He nodded. 'I can play with words, but it is possible they would be still alive without me. You're right to be angry. Please.' He gestured to the armchairs and reluctantly she sat down, placing the gun back in her bag, taking the wine glass he offered her.

'So why shouldn't I kill you?'

'Because it would be without purpose.' He sipped at his wine. 'I can understand why you wanted Novakovic dead—yes, Lucas told me about that, too: because he pulled the trigger. You wanted him dead because he was too professional; he didn't change his mind when he saw your family. I can understand also why you must kill the person who ordered the contract; it's only just. Me, I'm a middleman. My crime was to place together people who wanted to kill with people who could do it for them. I didn't think badly of your family; I just didn't think of them at all.'

'I'm not sure how that's meant to convince me.'

He smiled and said, 'I make a better argument in German.'

'You're German? I thought you were Hungarian.' She was annoyed with herself for asking; she didn't want detail, but she was curious all the same.

'No. I come from just outside Dresden, in the East. My wife was Hungarian.'

'Lucas said she died when she was young.'

'She didn't die: she was killed. Summer 1977. In one summer three women were raped and strangled. She was the second. They never found the killer, but after the summer, no more attacks.' He took a larger mouthful of wine. 'And yes, I'm seeing why you want me dead because that summer I wanted everyone dead. I wanted to kill policemen for doing nothing. I wanted to kill people for being happy. And all because I could not have what I most wanted: the killer killed.'

'I'm sorry.' She sipped at her wine too. This was what she'd least wanted—to see him as human, carrying his own sadness.

'But you still don't see why you're lucky. You *will* find your killer. You can make things right because you have Lucas and he will find them for you.'

She felt awkward hearing Lucas mentioned like that. He was the only person she could rely on and he'd helped her twice. But she was worried that he'd look upon her differently now that she'd lied to him and come here with a gun. For all she knew, though, this would lift her in his estimation, his skewed view of the world probably treating deceit as a virtue.

'You've known Lucas a long time?'

He shrugged but said, 'I guess as long as anybody. Almost long enough to be his friend.'

'Tell me about him.'

He finished the wine in his glass and poured himself another. 'What can I tell you about Lucas? First, don't be tricked by his accent. He's no Englishman. He's a Rhodesian.'

'A what?'

'Rhodesian,' he said, as if surprised by her ignorance. 'Rhodesia. You know, today's Zimbabwe. Before 1980 it was Rhodesia. That's where he comes from. All I know about his time there is he doesn't talk about it. Another thing: he says he doesn't speak any other language—it's a lie. He speaks a native African language, lots of . . .' He made a clicking noise with his tongue. 'You know? Sometimes when he was drunk he would speak like that for fun. A little Afrikaans too. That's where he went—South Africa, Namibia, Angola. He was very young when he left Rhodesia, before independence. I think he was only twenty-three when he came to Europe but he had a reputation already. I liked to work with him. He was good. Kill anyone. *He* would have killed your brother. He would have killed you.'

She couldn't process all the information that was coming at her. Lucas had been a rough sketch to her, a caricature at most, a man defined by his social awkwardness, his tics, and now Brodsky was suggesting a real and complex life. Lucas had come from somewhere, had grown up, possessed memories.

For the first time since meeting him, she felt like she wanted to get to know him, to see him open up about that past. And that desire made her sad too, because she was locked on a course that would put distance between them, almost certainly sending Lucas back into the shadows.

Because in the past, Lucas might have been willing to kill anyone, but he'd changed. He hadn't wanted to kill Novakovic; he didn't want to kill Brodsky. She could see now how he was fighting clear of that past and how she could only pull him back into it. It was beyond her control, though: the choice had been made for her by others, including the man sitting opposite, and she wouldn't rest until they'd all paid.

She had no doubt that Brodsky was good company, that he could tell her stories about Lucas. And he'd helped her with information. Perhaps he was a good person but so too had been the people whose deaths he'd arranged. She'd come here to kill him and she'd be guilty of betraying them if she didn't go through with it.

'So you lived here during the Communist era?'

'I lived my whole life in Communism. I was a Communist.'

'Tell me what it was like.'

'What do you want to know?'

She asked the right questions, kept him talking. She watched him drink while she tried desperately to think of a way to do this. A gun would have been easy but Lucas had denied her that. She didn't think she could stab him. Perhaps she could hit him with something.

All she had to do was wait until he'd drunk enough that his reactions would be slowed. She sipped at her own drink and allowed him to top it up, but Brodsky was drinking quickly and already seemed groggy when he got up for a second bottle.

'You didn't tell me how you came to Budapest,' she called out as he got the wine from the kitchen. She wasn't listening to his responses, her brain racing through its own internal dialogue, trying to think of a way to kill him but finding it hard to fix on that target. She was thinking about killing someone, ending a life.

He began to slow down and fell asleep before he'd finished the second bottle of wine. And there it was, offered up to her, but she still didn't know if she could do it. She walked over to the window, escaping the nausea and the confusion and the responsibility of who she was by looking down onto the empty street.

She'd been there for a few minutes when she heard someone call out, a monosyllable, nothing more, almost lost in the rustling of the trees. She struggled at first to see where it had come from and then noticed the boy standing down below on the opposite side of the street.

She felt an instant happy surge of recognition, only to have it sink away. It couldn't be Ben—of course it couldn't. He looked like him, though, even the way he was dressed, the apparition distant enough to cover up the flaws. Slowly, he lifted his arm in a wave. Her spine ran cold, a mixture of having been spotted and the boy's phantom resemblance to Ben. She lifted her own arm in response but then she heard another voice and dropped it.

She was embarrassed as she saw that someone was leaning out of a window in one of the neighboring apartments. Another teenager. He called a few more words to his friend before disappearing. The boy in the street hadn't seen her there. Nobody had seen her. Ben was dead. Brodsky had to die.

She closed the windows, the breeze putting up a half-hearted resistance. She walked into the kitchen without looking at him. There was no time for squeamishness; it would have to be a knife. She'd close her eyes, think about what he'd done, drive it into him. She could do it, and had to.

She opened a couple of drawers, the cutlery drawer rattling so noisily that she glanced into the living room to check that it hadn't disturbed him. As she turned again, her eyes were snagged by the cooker and she stared at it as she gently closed the drawer.

Gas. She could turn on the gas. She remembered someone telling her once that domestic gas wasn't poisonous. It was combustible, though, and that was a way of doing this without having to fall back on violence. And the death wouldn't look suspicious either. An accident, an act of God.

She walked back into the living room and carefully picked up one of the large lit candles, carried it into the kitchen and placed it on the work surface. She picked up her wine glass and washed it, then got her bag and took one last look at Brodsky, looking older now that he was asleep, and harmless.

She couldn't even know for certain that it would work but that made it better somehow, easier. Brodsky was guilty of killing her family, she believed that in her bones, but if this didn't kill him it would be like someone surviving the gallows or electric chair, an intervention by fate.

She turned on all the burners, a chorus of hissing, and left. She took the stairs, descending quickly, not knowing how long she had. She emerged from the building and slowed instinctively as she spotted the two boys chatting and smoking a short distance away. He didn't look as much like Ben from down there, his face harder and gaunt. He looked over and she turned her face from him.

She walked in the opposite direction, toward the illuminated backdrop of the parliament building, and at the end of the street she turned left, guessing that she was heading towards the river.

She was waiting, a timer ticking towards detonation in her head. It faltered, though, and she began to have her doubts, knowing all the while that it was too late to do anything about it.

If he'd woken up or if the candle had blown out, or if this was something that simply didn't work outside the world of the cinema, then she'd really made a mess of things, because Brodsky would know that she'd tried to kill him again and this time he might not be forgiving.

Then the noise came, hard to distinguish at first, like a fighter plane somewhere in the dark sky. It took shape, declaring itself unmistakably across the city: an explosion, some kind of alarm bell filling the void as it died down. Soon there'd be sirens and she was full of nervous excitement, her heart tripping like she was on speed.

She flagged down a taxi, relieved and exhilarated as she sat in the back for the short drive to the hotel. There were other feelings lurking in there, but she smothered them because she knew she had no reason to feel bad about Brodsky or going against Lucas.

It was a life that would be on her conscience but she was happy to carry it, no less so than if she'd been an executioner, carrying out the will of the state, ridding society of those who didn't deserve to live.

She felt confident, empowered, and then she got back to the hotel and immediately stumbled into herself, her triumphalism crumbling guiltily around her. Lucas was sitting in the lobby, clearly waiting for her, his seat positioned so that he could see anyone coming into the hotel. She waved as soon as she saw him, trying to look cheerful, like someone who'd been out seeing the city, knowing she couldn't conceal what he half knew already.

Lucas waved back and smiled a little but by the time she reached him, he looked stern again and said, 'Take a seat. There's something I need to tell you.' She sat down, still trying to look innocent. 'I spent the evening making a few calls, looking into the information Bruno gave us. I discovered something very interesting about the ownership of Larsen Grohl.'

It took her a second or two to realize this talk was nothing to do with her visit to Brodsky. She couldn't understand why he hadn't mentioned it when he clearly knew she'd been there, but then she added it all up, that he hadn't mentioned it because this was more important, whatever it was he'd found out, the ownership of Larsen Grohl.

'Why? Who owns it?'

'You do.'

'What? I don't get it.'

He nodded, his face somber as he said, 'It's one of your father's companies. It means the person who murdered your family wasn't some enemy from the past; it was someone on the inside, someone in a position to use company funds and a company account to do something like this.'

She still couldn't quite grasp what he was saying, except that he'd been right, that someone her dad had trusted had plotted to have him killed. Someone within Larsen Grohl had used her dad's own money to have him and his family murdered.

A siren sounded as some emergency vehicle sped past the hotel. Lucas seemed oblivious, so she said, 'We need to speak to Simon, find out the names of all employees of Larsen Grohl, past and present, find out if any of them had grudges.'

'It's more straightforward than that. We just need to find out who authorized the payment.' He looked uncomfortable, like he wanted to say something else but wasn't sure how to broach it.

'What is it?'

'For the time being at least, it's probably best if you don't speak to Simon about this.'

'Why not?' She answered herself, laughing as she said, 'You don't seriously think he had anything to do with this?'

'He had the most to gain.'

'You don't know Simon. And think about it: if he did this to get his hands on the business, what about me? I'm still alive, and I have the business now. He even knows I've left it to him in my will, so . . . Why am I still here? If it's him, why am I still here?'

'Biding his time? If anything, that could explain why the threat to you disappeared: because you were too close—it would have raised suspicions. As it is, you've given him free rein to run the business and he can wait until the opportunity arises.'

She shook her head. 'No, you're wrong. I trust Simon totally.'

'Do you?' He stared at her quizzically, like he knew something about her that she didn't know herself. Another piercing siren sounded and this time Lucas glanced briefly towards the lobby doors before saying, 'So he knows about me, does he? He knows you're here in Budapest? He knows what you're doing?'

She didn't respond because she knew how it looked and that she had no explanation for it. She'd wanted to keep Lucas to herself, to keep this whole business to herself, but not because she hadn't trusted Simon. She wasn't even sure why she'd wanted things like that except, perhaps, the belief that revenge was her responsibility, and that she hadn't wanted it taken away from her, the only thing left that she could do for them.

Lucas seemed to notice that she was upset because he softened now and said, 'Look, I'm not saying it's your uncle. I'm just trying to keep you safe and prepare you for all possibilities. We'll find out, then you can tell him. In the meanwhile, you have to make like nothing's happened.'

She nodded and said, 'I hope it isn't him.'

'I know.' He paused for a second or two. 'Get some sleep. I'm getting the early train to Vienna so I'll see you in a couple of days.'

'Okay.' A third siren grew sickeningly louder and she began to get nervous, wondering how bad the explosion had been.

Lucas looked to the lobby doors. 'Must be a fire.' He stood up and said, 'Ella, don't worry about this evening, and don't worry about Simon. You're right, I don't know him.'

She offered him a lackluster smile. It couldn't be Simon. She did know him, and even without that lifetime of accumulated knowledge, the way he'd idolized her dad, doted on Ben, she couldn't believe the person who'd taken her so protectively under his wing this summer had conspired to kill them.

And yet. And yet there was a single discordant note sounding through her thoughts. She tried to dismiss it but she wanted to get back to London to make sure, check that she hadn't simply overlooked it.

The folder he'd given her was still in her hotel room, a strange menagerie of companies, their profiles full of arcane language, some of them based in remote and exotic locations, but nowhere among them could she remember seeing the name of Larsen Grohl. She was trying to think of a reason why he might not have included it, but she could think of only one, and she was afraid.

Chapter Sixteen

She had no idea she was being followed. He'd be able to follow her right up to the door, push her inside. It had always amazed him, the number of targets who, whether through innocence, ignorance or complacency, behaved like there was nothing for them to be afraid of.

Ella reached her room, but even as she took out her key and slid it into the lock, she didn't think to look behind her. She became aware of him for the first time as he stepped through the doorway with her.

Startled, she jumped backwards, too late, and said, 'Jesus fucking Christ, Lucas—you scared the shit out of me!' She gathered her thoughts a little and said, 'You said a couple of days. And why didn't you call first?' The momentum was building again. 'And Jesus, what's with creeping up behind me like that?'

He closed the door and looked around the room. She could have had a suite, a whole floor, but here she was in a regular double. He liked that; it reminded him of who she was, who he'd first met, and almost made him regret why he was here.

'If I'd been sent here to kill you—simple, you'd be dead. And you better start thinking about that, about being aware, taking extra precautions.'

Her anger sank back like a little child's as she said, 'You think I'm in . . .' He put his hand up, fighting to control his own anger.

'You're a player now! You killed Bruno Brodsky! You don't do things like that and go back to being sweet little Ella Hatto. You're a player and you need security. You get that? Your old life is over!'

She sat down on the edge of the bed. For a moment, he thought she was about to tell him that her old life had ended back in Italy but instead, her voice sounding small, she said, 'I had to kill him. I'm sorry.'

Lucas felt like the apology was aimed directly at him, rather than being the remorse of a passion murderer; she'd already become colder than that, like someone following a set of instructions in the avenger's handbook with no sense of the implications.

'You had to kill him? What about the three other people who died? What about the two-year-old boy in the hospital who now has no mother or grandmother? You had to kill them too?' She looked shocked and began to say something but he preempted her. 'Please, you're not that stupid. You blow up a building, people die.' She started to weep, but he couldn't bring himself to feel sorry for her. He'd seen her cry before and it had left him pained, embarrassed because she'd been brought down by a love and loss he couldn't have imagined. Now, though, she was crying for herself, and he suspected that those deaths in Budapest meant even less to her than they did to him.

Maybe a lot less, because at least they left him questioning his own part in bringing them about. If he'd killed Bruno for her, he'd have saved the others, one unjust death instead of four. That was a false logic, though. He could see that. The only way he could have avoided any of it was never to have helped her in the first place.

She looked up at him and said, 'What will happen now?'

He wasn't sure what she was asking about but he wanted to get on with the business at hand. 'Dan's checking out Larsen Grohl. Once he has something he'll come and see you. I've paid him a retainer to see this through but if you want to use his services after that—and I do recommend him—you'll have to discuss a financial arrangement. That's everything.'

She looked confused, then accusatory as she said, 'What, that's it? I make one mistake and you're turning your back on me?'

'You didn't make a mistake. You knew exactly what you were doing.'

'And who are you to condemn me for it?'

'I don't condemn you. We're just heading in different directions.' He wanted to add something else, to offer some words of friendship, but he could think of nothing, and wanted simply to be away from her, from all of this.

'Go then.' Her eyes were full of bitterness. 'Before you're tainted.'

He nodded, but stopped at the door. 'I wish you well, Ella, but if I ever see you again I'll treat you as a threat, and if anyone makes an attempt on my life, I'll come looking for you. Just so you know where we stand.'

She looked hurt, but she was dangerous now, and unpredictable. It was in her eyes, the deadness of loss replaced by a blinkered determination. He'd seen it in other people plenty of times, had extinguished it often enough, and he didn't want to be there to see what it made of her. He had to leave now, while there might still be reasons *to* leave.

He took a cab across town to Dan's flat and found him cooking something complicated, his gun within easy reach of the chopping board. It made him smile to see Dan, the ultimate postmodern hitman, every move, every outfit and lifestyle choice informed by the books he'd read and the films he'd seen.

There had always been fantasists, of course, but that was the difference with Dan, because he could actually do the business. That was what amused him, knowing that the placing of the gun was an act, a stylistic touch; that Dan wouldn't have needed it to fight off any would-be assailants.

Lucas looked at the array of chopped ingredients and the meat he was expertly slicing, and said, 'Expecting company?'

Dan shook his head and said, 'This is how I relax. Want some?'

'No, thanks. I'm flying back in a couple of hours.'

'You're really going for it?'

'Yes. No more favors. The old Lucas is dead.'

Dan smiled and said, 'Lucky for you, mate, he left you all his money.' Lucas laughed. 'So, how did she take it?'

'Oh, you know.' He stared at Dan's nimble handiwork with the knife and after a few seconds he said, 'Help her as far as you can, but take my advice: once this job is done, make your excuses.'

'Think she's gonna turn psycho or something?'

'I don't know, just a bad feeling. Truth is, it's probably just me. I'm turning soft.'

Dan smiled again and said, 'Well, you're bloody old, mate.'

'True. So long, Dan. I'll save a place for you in the rest home.'

'Reckon they need a cook?'

He walked a short way along the street before hailing a cab for Heathrow. On the way to the airport, he realized he was in a good mood, content, even happy. He'd removed himself from Ella Hatto before any lasting damage had been done and could look upon it all now as a useful reminder of why he wanted no more to do with this closed world.

He wanted to live like other people. In forty-two years he'd had only the briefest taste of what that was like. He didn't even know if he had the necessary components to live like that, if he was too damaged. But he considered himself lucky, because he had a chance to find out. And as long as he was alive, it was never too late.

Chapter Seventeen

She'd been venturing less into the hotel's public spaces, and even today she'd waited until they'd called up from the front desk to tell her he was here. He was in the lobby. She hadn't seen him since that day with Novakovic but he was unmistakable in his black suit and shirt.

'How's it going?'

'Fine, thanks. Let's go through to the bar.' She led him through and sat down.

The waiter approached with a smile and she said, 'Mineral water, please, Malvern. Sparkling. Dan?'

He looked at his watch before saying, 'I'll have a Talisker, straight up.' He smiled at Ella then. He looked too conspicuously attractive for his line of work. 'Mainly here to say hello, touch base, that sort of thing.'

'You *are* a hitman, aren't you?' He looked around but she already knew no one was within earshot.

'That title's a bit restrictive.'

'You'll kill the people I want you to kill?'

'Oh yeah, no worries. I don't want you thinking I'm a thug with a gun, that's all.'

She smiled. 'I don't, but speaking of thugs, I need some security, minders.'

'No you don't. Minders are for celebrities. Anyway, you're not in any danger, are you?'

'I don't know. I killed Bruno Brodsky. Lucas told me I should start watching my back.'

'Ah, I wouldn't worry about that. It's just his way of saying you should be careful who you kill.'

She took in what he'd said, feeling cheated and angry, thinking Lucas had used Brodsky as an excuse. She realized then that he'd acted on principle, and that was harder to take. Hers was a just cause and yet she was being shunned by a man whose life had been littered with unimaginable violence.

'What's the problem with Lucas?'

'He's run his course, that's all. He wants out.'

The waiter came with the drinks. Dan put his nose into the glass and breathed in deeply, looking intoxicated by the smell alone when he surfaced. He took a sip then and said, 'Wanna hear a story about how good Lucas was in his day?'

'Okay.'

'Right. About six years ago, Lucas got a contract on a guy called Cheval, or Chavanne. Chavanne, that's it. Now he'd done a bit of work with Chavanne, liked him, so he called to say he was on his way, give him a chance to put his house in order. Chavanne asked if there was any way out, Lucas told him there wasn't, Chavanne thanks him for the call. Then he takes a bucket-load of pills.'

'Why didn't he run?'

'Because he knew Lucas would find him. And Lucas, cocky bastard, knew that too—that's why he called.' He took another sip of his drink. 'Here's the best bit, though. Whether Chavanne didn't wanna do Lucas out of his fee, who knows, but he left a note saying something along the lines of, 'L is coming. I'm a dead man. This is the better way out,' that kind of thing. The French papers got a hold of it and loved it. Who was this mysterious L who could instill so much fear that a man would kill himself rather than face him? That was how good Lucas was—so good he didn't even have to do anything. No wonder he turned so bloody existential.'

'That's an interesting story.' She wondered if it was just that—a story, like the ones that Brodsky and Lucas had told her.

She didn't have any way of knowing what was true, who could be trusted, who were her enemies. But she had to put her faith in someone and now that person was Dan, who'd been chosen by Lucas, who'd been chosen by her father, and even his whole life had been a lie to her. 'What have you found out?'

'Nothing much yet but I'm tracking a couple of potential contacts. That's the problem for companies like Larsen Grohl: they have to employ people, and people are bloody unreliable. Give me another week or two and I'll have something.'

'Okay.' She took a token sip from her drink and got up to leave. He looked taken aback that she was going already but she didn't want to get to know him, not even as well as she'd known Lucas. 'Please, stay and finish your drink.'

She signed the bill and walked back out into the lobby. She'd almost reached the elevator when she heard her name called behind her. It startled her, a flashback, but even when she identified the voice she felt uneasy. She turned to see him walking towards her.

'Simon. What brings you here?'

'Oh, just thought I'd stop by. Haven't seen you in a few days.'

She glanced over to the entrance of the bar, smiling as she said, 'Good. Shall we have coffee in the Thames Foyer? I'm growing tired of the bar.'

He laughed and as they walked, he said, 'Are you okay? You look . . . I don't know.'

'I'm fine. You calling my name like that spooked me, that's all. The gunman in Florence, he called out my name.'

'Oh, God, I'm sorry.'

'Don't be silly.' They sat and had coffee and as they talked, she became more convinced that he had to be innocent, and was even tempted to ask him about Larsen Grohl, backing off only because she didn't want him to think she'd been snooping around behind his back.

Even so, he seemed to pick up that something was wrong and asked her a couple of times if she was sure she was okay, saying finally, 'You know, you've been living in a hotel for too long, that's what it is. Bound to get you down, living in a place like this.'

'Simon, there's nothing wrong with me, honestly. And believe me, this is a great place to live.'

'I'd still be happier if you came home and lived with us, just until you get a place of your own.' He stood to leave, but said casually, 'I called by on . . . Was it Tuesday? Thursday? They said you'd gone away for a couple of days.'

A silent alarm sounded but it was too late. She was panicked because she hadn't covered her tracks, and more so because she couldn't work out whether his inquiry was innocuous or a trap. Caught out in the open, she smiled a little and told him the truth.

'I went to Budapest.' Simon's smile dropped and she seized the initiative, saying, 'There's nothing wrong with that, is there?'

'No, not at all. Did you go alone?'

'Yeah. Chris and I were gonna go there during the summer. I just decided to go on a whim. To be honest, I shouldn't have bothered.'

He nodded, but in some subtle way she sensed that he didn't believe her.

She was trying to read him but suddenly he seemed relaxed again as he said, 'Traveling alone's never much fun.' He smiled.

'This week's project—get out there and get a boyfriend!' He kissed her on the cheek and left.

She strolled back through the lobby, troubled by the way Simon had managed to walk right up behind her without her noticing. She went to the reception desk and arranged to be moved into a suite that afternoon; from now on, she'd talk business behind closed doors.

She started counting the days then, waiting for Dan to get in touch. But a couple of days after moving into the suite, reception called and told her there was someone to see her, a Miss Welsh. Ella tried to sound light-hearted as she asked them to send her up, as if Vicky Welsh were an old friend. She didn't want the hotel staff knowing that she was being visited by the police.

It was bad timing, too. She guessed the investigation had finally unearthed something, and a few weeks before, she would have been grateful for that, but it seemed like an irrelevance now. Whatever the breakthrough, she wouldn't let it get in the way of what she was doing.

To Ella's relief, Vicky Welsh was wearing a trouser suit and looked more like a businesswoman than a policewoman. She was friendly, refused the offer of a drink, commented on the room, asked Ella how she'd been.

But as she sat down, she said, 'I just wanted to ask you some questions, if you don't mind. Just on an informal basis.'

'Of course.' She took out a notebook and Ella said, 'You did say informal?'

'Yes, informal in the legal sense. I just need to clarify some facts.'

Ella's thoughts were struggling to catch up—there hadn't been a breakthrough: she was being questioned.

'Well, I'm more than happy to help if I can.' The sound of her own words grated; she was beginning to sound like Simon.

Vicky Welsh gave a pinched smile. 'Let me see. I understand you went to Budapest last week?'

'Yeah.'

'Business or pleasure?'

'Pleasure.' Ella was suddenly conscious of the muscles in her face, of the blood prickling beneath the surface of her skin. 'Uh, it was one of the places we were gonna go in the summer. So I went.'

'Does the name Bruno Brodsky mean anything to you?'

Ella shook her head. Vicky Welsh stared at her, the scrutiny unnerving her further.

'I'm not sure I follow what's going on here. I assumed this was about my family. If it isn't, perhaps you should tell me what it *is* about.'

Vicky Welsh nodded, but wrote something else in her notebook before responding. 'Maybe it is about your family. Stephen Lucas was staying in the same hotel in Budapest at the same time as you. I take it you've heard of *him*?'

Ella could tell from her face and from the tone of the question that it was pointless denying it. Having seen how spineless Chris was, she guessed he'd probably given them Lucas's name right at the start.

'Yeah, I met Lucas while I was there. He lives in Europe; it seemed like a good opportunity to catch up, thank him.' She was feeling more combative now, and sensed her guilt was less physically manifest as a result. 'And yes, I lied about not knowing his name the last time I saw you.'

'Why?'

'Because he asked me to. The man saved my life.'

Vicky Welsh nodded and looked momentarily sympathetic, but quickly reverted to business. 'Stephen Lucas knew Bruno Brodsky, and Brodsky was a fixer, the kind of person who could have arranged the hit on your family. It seems a huge coincidence, then, that during the flying visit you and Lucas made to Budapest, Bruno Brodsky was killed in a huge gas explosion.'

'I told you, I don't know anyone called Bruno Brodsky.' She couldn't imagine they had anything more than the circumstantial evidence of her being in Budapest with Lucas, and that made her bolder. 'You've already said that Lucas knew him, and I assume you know something about Lucas's background. So why don't you go and speak to him?'

'As I said, this isn't a formal inquiry.' She looked uncomfortable and clearly didn't want to answer the question. It made Ella wonder if Lucas was protected in some way. 'However, I have to warn you, Ella, this and other matters are being investigated vigorously. You may or may not be aware of it, but some of the people around you have a questionable relationship with the law—you'd do well not to be too influenced by them.'

'Don't worry; I'm not being influenced by anybody.'

Vicky Welsh nodded, but seemed disappointed.

It was only when she was left alone again that Ella's nerves ran wild. She started to sweat, her heart beating erratically. It wasn't even that she was afraid of being caught, but she felt sick with fear at the prospect of them getting to her before her job was done.

Everything seemed to be closing in on her. If the police knew about Budapest, others would know too, the kind of people Lucas had warned her about. Maybe even Simon was beginning to suspect her of something. And she couldn't understand what was taking Dan so long. She wanted him to be as conscious as she was that time was running out.

Chapter Eighteen

It was another week before Dan got in touch. There were no progress reports, no contact of any kind, and then he called her from the lobby and told her that he had someone with him she'd really like to meet. A few minutes later they were standing facing each other in the sitting room of her suite.

Dan was wearing his usual lethal styling but the guy with him was dressed in sloppy jeans and a hoodie. He was quite young but it was hard to see it through the long scruffy hair and what looked like the uncertain beginnings of a beard.

She felt her body tighten uneasily with the thought that this wasn't some associate of Dan's but the employee with a grudge she'd hoped for. He looked like he could fit that bill but she didn't want it to be him. The guy in front of her was too unassuming, too inconsequential, to have caused her this much pain, to be deserving of the wrath she would have to direct at him.

'Take a seat, Jim.' Dan smiled at her then, dispelling her fears as he said, 'Don't worry, he's a friendly.'

'Jim Catesby. How do you do?' He shook her hand before taking a seat.

'Pleased to meet you.' She turned to Dan and said, 'I take it you found something?'

'My mate Jim, that's what I found. Works for Larsen Grohl, testing computer security, as luck would have it. But provenance first. Jim, tell Ella how you got your job.'

Jim cleared his throat and said, 'Of course, yeah. Summer I finished college, couple of years ago, I was flying home from Chicago—my dad lives out there. Anyway, I got bumped off my flight so they put me on the next one and upgraded me to first class. That's how I ended up sitting next to your dad.'

'My dad?' It saddened her suddenly to hear a stranger saying he'd known him.

'That's right. We talked a lot on the way back, mainly about computers, the Internet, security, and I was telling him about the hacking we did at college. He was really interested in that bit. Anyway, by the time we touched down he'd offered me a job. I couldn't believe my luck: a cool job, good money, all from talking to a guy on a plane. I only met him a few times after that but he was always interested in what I was doing, you know, not just at work, but like, my life. He was a cool guy. I'm really sorry he's dead.'

'Thank you.' It made her want to cry because it reminded her of the kind of man her dad had been.

Dan sat forward now and said, 'Obviously, in theory, Jim here could be lying but the one other person I spoke to at the company seemed to back up his story, and anyway, I'd know if he was lying.'

'So would I,' said Ella. 'So where's this going?'

'I gave him the info Lucas gave me, to see what he could do with it.'

He gestured towards Jim, who hesitantly took over the telling of the story, saying, 'Yeah, the account you're talking about was marked for external relations.'

'What does that mean?'

'I don't know. It's just the name they attached to it. The only people with access to it were your dad and your uncle. I did some unauthorized digging—which, I stress, is something I wouldn't normally do.' She waved away his concern. 'Your dad was the one who used the account. Last year, for example, he'd used it five times, then once in January of this year. Your uncle hadn't used it in eighteen months, but this June he used it to make two payments.'

She heard the words like she'd been punched in the face with them.

'Is it possible someone else pretended to be my uncle?'

'Theoretically. I could have done it, a couple of other people if they'd been determined and lucky enough not to get caught. In other words, no.'

She looked at Dan and said, 'Does he know what this is all about?'

'The basics.'

'So you know what you're telling me, that my uncle killed my family?'

'That's how it looks, I know.' On the verge of saying something else, he halted, then built up the courage again. 'Your dad and your uncle, they always seemed to get on well enough but your uncle was always very much the sidekick. The feeling at LG was that he resented that, felt undervalued.' Jim's earlier doubts appeared to resurface now and he added, 'I'm not saying that explains anything. I resent my brother but I wouldn't kill him. I'd probably risk my life for him.'

Ella nodded. She'd never noticed any bad feeling between Simon and her dad, but then she'd managed to live for twenty years knowing almost nothing about her own family, how it did business, its wealth and where it had come from.

She thought of Ben, too, wondering if he'd resented her. Perhaps it was the prerogative of the younger child to resent the elder, just for being first, for gaining freedom and privilege ahead of them. It made her wish she'd given him more time in the last couple of years, shown more interest, as pointless as it was to wish for something like that.

'Thanks for your help, Jim. It won't go unrewarded.'

'That's not why I did it.'

'I know. Dan, could you show Jim back down to the lobby and then come back.'

She shook hands with Jim and closed the door behind them. Her thoughts piled up into a sprawling and confused wreckage. She felt like she should be screaming, tearing the room up, that her heart should be spilling out in pieces on the floor, but she could muster none of it. It was as if her spirit had been hardening unnoticed, growing colder, and now at the moment of truth, there was no passion left within her.

Dan knocked and came back in, saying as soon as he sat down, 'So, you want me to kill him?'

She nodded. 'But we have to do this carefully. I need to think it through.'

'Are you okay?' She shrugged and he said, 'Well, you just found out your uncle had your family killed, tried to kill you.'

'Strange, isn't it? I didn't think I'd feel like this either.' She laughed. 'It's funny, they protected me my whole life from the truth of what they did and yet, after one summer, here I am thinking about killing Simon—no doubts, no soul-searching, no reservations. What's become of me? Surely I should feel something.'

She felt a sudden urge to look in a mirror, to see whether she recognized the person looking back at her. The Ella Hatto she'd been would have felt something, but her memory of that person was unsound, like a dream or like the unformed memories of early childhood.

'You do want me to kill him?'

'Of course. How could I do otherwise? If I didn't see justice done I'd feel like I'd sanctioned the death of my own family.'

'Too right. That's how I'd feel.'

'Do you have any brothers or sisters?'

'Kid sister. She's a marine biologist.' He seemed full of pride for a moment, then regretful as he said, 'Were you and your brother close?'

'I don't know. It's the kind of closeness you take for granted, isn't it?'

'Yeah, I know what you mean.'

'I think that's why it upsets me so much. He got killed at the one time in our lives when we really didn't know very much about each other.'

'It's a real bloody shame.' He appeared genuinely saddened, displaying a warmth that Ella found attractive. As she looked at him, she thought of asking more about his own family but stopped herself, realizing it would be a mistake. Lucas had taught her that lesson: there were no real friendships in this business.

'I've agreed to spend Christmas in the Caribbean with Simon.'

'That's good. People get murdered all the time out there. Very low detection rate.'

'He owns a house on the shore on Saint Peter. He's got his own boat, too. One year, we rented a house just along the coast and they came over in the boat.' He was smiling at her and she got the impression he was hearing a reminiscence, not the foundation of a plan. 'I'll be able to speak to him on the phone but I know I won't be able to look him in the face. So I'll call him, tell him I'm going traveling, but that I'll be in Saint Peter for Christmas. I'll try to rent the same house, for old times' sake, you know? Then I'll invite him over and he'll come in the boat. That should give us plenty of opportunities, shouldn't it? A boat?'

Dan finally caught up with her but tried to sound like he'd followed her from the start as he said, 'Oh yeah, too right! Especially if he doesn't know I'm there. One thing, though.'

'What?'

'Like I said, the Caribbean's a good place to make someone disappear. So we're gonna have to be pretty damn careful we don't give him the opportunity to make you disappear first. We need to cover our tracks but do it in a way that doesn't make him suspicious.'

'He knows I was in Budapest.'

'Ah.' He looked stumped for a second before saying, 'Does he know why?'

'He knows when, and by now he must know what happened when I was there.' She was tempted to mention the visit from Vicky Welsh, but was afraid that Dan would back out altogether if he knew the police were closing in on her.

'Even if he doesn't suspect, that could rattle him enough to force his hand. So we really do need to take care. At the same time, I'll get Jim to spread some misinformation. If he thinks for a minute that you killed Bruno, he'll never take the bait.'

She'd had her doubts about Dan, but she could see now that he was smart and that she could almost certainly trust him, for the time being anyway. He was being cautious—part of his job, she supposed—but Ella believed unquestioningly that he'd deliver Simon into her hands.

'There are some things I'll need to do before leaving but I want to go soon. A few days, no more.'

'Suits me. I'll need some time on the ground out there anyway.' It was decided, and she could see no other possibility than that it would happen. The details would take some working out but the fundamentals were fixed, written in stone, as if it had always been so, as if she'd been born to fulfill this role.

Two days later she rented a car and drove home. She was tempted to drive by the house but didn't. She couldn't bear to look at it, to see the signs of another family living there, occupying the rooms her family had lived in.

Instead she drove to the village church. It was a small place but it still took her a while to get her bearings and find their graves. Two new ones had already been added since and she glanced at their flower-decked plots before standing at the foot of her own.

Two simple wooden crosses, one for her parents, one on the neighboring grave for Ben. The gravestones would be on within the month but she almost preferred it like this, the bare facts of their names on the little metal plates pinned into the wood, no sentiments declared.

The turned soil was half lost in fallen leaves, the boundaries merging with the surrounding grass, an integral part of the church-yard with its trees and hedgerows, its crows' chorus in the hollow autumn air. She'd never imagined it being important, where a person was buried, but she was glad they were here.

Someone had put a bunch of red carnations at the foot of Ben's cross. They were beginning to die off now but she guessed they'd only been there a short time. It saddened her to think of someone else grieving in isolation, unknown to her; it made her realize again how little she'd known him at the end.

But it was too late for regrets, too late for wishing she'd known them better. Nothing she could say or do now would make any difference. These gentle mounds of earth would sink a little more, the past would grow a little more distant, its precise details blurring.

The day would come when she wouldn't be able to remember her mother's infectious laugh, or the way Ben told a joke, all self-conscious and constantly correcting himself, or the skeptical smile he'd throw at people when he thought they were teasing him.

For now, those things still seemed in the present, but she knew she wouldn't be able to hold onto them.

She wasn't sure how long she'd been standing there, fifteen minutes perhaps, when she realized there was someone else in the churchyard. She turned, expecting to see someone visiting another grave. It was a girl, standing some twenty yards off, staring at her.

She was wearing jeans and a short duffel coat, a bunch of red carnations in her hand. She looked about Ben's age; she was pretty. When she realized Ella had seen her, she looked around nervously, like she wanted to run.

'Hello,' said Ella.

The girl moved closer. 'I'm sorry. I didn't mean to disturb you.'

'Not at all. Please.' The girl came the rest of the way. 'I'm Ella Hatto, Ben's sister.' She pointed at the flowers and said, 'I'm guessing that's who you came to see.'

'I hope you don't mind. I was at school with him. We were friends.'

'I don't mind at all. I'm glad someone else remembers him, thinks of him.'

'Oh, a lot of us do. I don't think anyone else comes here but . . .' She appeared to have second thoughts about finishing the sentence and said, 'I'm sorry. I'm Alice Shaw.'

'Were you and Ben . . . ?'

'No.' She was insistent, embarrassed, but went on, 'I liked him, a lot. A few people thought he liked me, but we never, I mean . . . There's no point in speculating. We were friends.' Her face choked up with emotion.

'I'm sure he would have liked you. I know it.'

Alice smiled but her eyes filled quickly with tears. One ran a rapid course down her cheek and she wiped it away. 'Sorry.'

'Don't be.' Ella took a step forward and held her, surprised by how tightly Alice held her back, and by the tears that flowed from the girl, as if this were the first time anyone had given her permission to express her loss.

And for all she knew, her loss was even greater than Ella's. She thought of Joyce's *The Dead*, of Gretta Conroy still mourning the long-lost love of her youth, and then she thought of Lucas, wanting to ask him if he'd read it, feeling a loss herself that she would never be able to do so.

For another twenty minutes or so, she and Alice talked through their memories of Ben. She walked back with her then to the small parking lot. And as she drove away, Ella tried to sort her thoughts and feelings into a pattern that made sense. It was a puzzle that had troubled her nearly every day and there was only ever one clear way out of the maze—vengeance.

For the first few months, that need had been focused on the imagined shadowy figure who'd done this to her family. That figure had taken on a form now, a name and a face, all too familiar, but the need remained the same, and if anything, her resolution was firmer.

And now she knew something else too. As she thought of Ben and Alice, imagining them together, imagining the whole cycle of their relationship being played out, and all the others that might have lain ahead, she understood for the first time the full cruelty of the act she was avenging.

The pain he'd caused them wasn't just the pain she felt, but the pain that Alice Shaw felt, the pain of everything that had been buried in that churchyard, and even if it was the last thing she did, she'd return it to him in full, every last ounce of it.

Chapter Nineteen

The day had stretched beyond itself, her nerves eating away at each other. It was the waiting; she'd waited six months and yet this final day, in sight of her goal, was the hardest to bear. It felt like her heart had slowed, her blood thickened.

Dan had seemed perfectly at ease, sitting out on the terrace with a drink, an air of repose like he'd gone into some sort of meditative trance. It had come as a relief when he'd finally stirred midway through the afternoon and headed off to take up his position down at the jetty.

An hour later he'd phoned to say he'd spotted the boat and time had notched down another gear. It had been at least thirty minutes now, and she was beginning to worry—that something had gone wrong, that Simon had seen through her plan, that Dan had double-crossed her.

She walked around, trying to glimpse the jetty from the upstairs windows, even though she knew it was out of sight, checking her appearance in the mirror, stopping at the sound of imagined noises.

The stillness in the house was eerie. At first she'd put it down to its emptiness, the fact that the staff were all off for the night, that there was no one else around. But the silence was total: no birdsong or insect noise. She'd heard plenty of times about the way nature paused before hurricanes, earthquakes, and that's how it felt, like a portent.

Finally, the phone rang, so loud against this supernatural hush that it startled her and she had to let it ring a few times to get her composure back. It was Dan, cheery and unconcerned. 'Okay, we're ready for you.'

'See you in a minute.' She hung up the phone and walked over to the mirror again before walking out and through the gardens. She was trying not to think about what he'd meant by that—*we're ready for you*—telling herself he'd meant nothing at all, that it was just the way he spoke.

Something wasn't right, though, something she couldn't put her finger on, the stillness like an omen. It was hot and the sun hadn't set but that stillness was skewing everything like a dream. Only the tops of the tall palms were finding any movement in the air.

Clouds were stacking up on the horizon. They'd bring an early dusk, and as she reached the jetty and saw the boat, she felt the first touch of the developing breeze. Maybe that was it, a storm, and she wanted a storm. It would help them and seemed right for what was about to happen.

She could already see Dan on the deck, leaning nonchalantly against the open door, wearing his beach shirt and surf shorts. She'd never seen him look less like a hitman. He smiled and waved with his gun as she got close.

Stepping aboard, she noticed the boat rocking gently, the beginnings of a swell. Dan looked through the open door into the lounge, checking on the captives, then took a step towards Ella and spoke quietly.

'Bit of a problem. He's gone and brought the whole family with him.'

'I know.'

'Oh. Well, I put the kids in the front cabin so they don't see you. I guessed you'd wanna do the wife. I mean, we have to, really; you don't know how much she knows.'

'Of course.' She was glad she'd kept Dan in the dark on the full scale of her plans. He could bail out on her once this was done but she hadn't wanted him following Lucas before she'd had her retribution. 'Did you have any problems?'

He shrugged and said, 'I had to give him a crack. I told them not to do anything stupid but he tried one on.'

She nodded and walked into the lounge, hot and airless even with the air conditioning. Simon and Lucy were sitting on one of the long cushioned seats, hands and feet bound, gagged. Lucy looked briefly hopeful and then confused at the sight of Ella, the first hint that she'd known nothing about it. Simon had a wound on the side of his head, the cheek run with blood. He didn't look surprised when he saw her, just resigned.

Dan had followed her in and she said, 'Take his gag off. Just his.'

She thought Simon might say something as soon as he was free but he didn't, staring at her instead, inviting her to go first. It was the first time she'd seen him since finding out the truth and she'd expected to see something different in him. He looked as benign as ever, though, and if anything, wore an expression that suggested he was the one who'd been betrayed.

'Why did you do it, Simon?'

'Why did I do what, exactly?'

She glanced at Lucy, whose eyes still pleaded for an explanation, then back to Simon. 'Lucas found Novakovic, who, in case you're wondering, is the guy you paid to kill my family, *your* family.'

Lucy looked at him in horror. He shook his head. 'You're mistaken, Ella, or you've been led astray by these people. I've never heard that name before in my life.'

'No, because you dealt with Bruno Brodsky, and he hired Novakovic, just like he hired the men who came for me in Italy. You thought you dealt with Brodsky anonymously but he'd dealt with that account before and recognized it from his records. Larsen Grohl, a company you neglected to tell me I own. Only two people had the authority to use that account: you and Dad. Dad hadn't used it since January. You made two payments in June.'

'This is ridiculous. Even these names—it's all ridiculous. You're wrong.'

'No, I'm right. And if Dad hadn't hired Lucas to protect me you would have got away with it. If you'd engineered an accident for me in the last six months you'd have got away with it. But you didn't and now I've caught up with you. Just tell me why you did it.'

He shook his head slowly and said, 'Ella, I didn't do anything.' He laughed to himself, saying, 'How can I give you a reason for something I know absolutely nothing about?'

That laugh was the first chink in the armor, a window on the lie, a suggestion of the person he had to be to have done this. She latched onto it, drawing strength from it, and said to Dan, 'Bring the kids out.'

Simon looked suddenly confused, too shocked to respond. Dan said, 'You sure?' She nodded and he made a move but then turned to Simon and said, 'Mate, just tell her why you did it.'

'Fuck you!' It was aimed at Dan, but with Lucy crying out through her gag, he looked at Ella and said, 'Ella, please . . .'

'Dan, get the kids.'

Dan handed her the gun and left.

Lucy was trying to catch Ella's eye, but Ella was looking directly at Simon, desperately searching his face for an indication of what was on his mind. She couldn't believe she'd been fooled by him, that they'd all been so fooled. He had a slight defiant smile on his lips now, but she had the feeling it didn't mean anything, that it was just a strange side effect of the shock he was in.

Dan came back in with George and Harry, gagged, hands bound in front of them. He was shepherding them like he was a nursery school teacher. Harry was old enough to know something was wrong and looked fearful at the sight of her there with a gun. George looked excited, though, as if in seeing her he'd suddenly realized it was all a game.

She said to Simon, 'Clearly, you didn't care about your brother, his wife, his children, but what about your own children, Simon? Tell me why you did it or I'll have him kill them right now.'

Lucy pleaded through her gag to Simon and it seemed to be in response to her that he eventually said, 'Okay, okay!' He looked back at Ella with a certain righteous defiance, like a man defending himself in court. 'Ella, you've been through a lot, I can see that, but please, I'm begging you to see reason now. I don't care what other people have told you. Listen to me. I didn't kill them.'

'You don't get it. Lying to me won't save them. Tell me why you did it!'

'I didn't do anything!' He produced a sudden burst of violent energy, his body buckling and straining against his bindings. Dan bristled, ready to make a move, but Simon calmed again and stared at her accusingly. 'You're sick, Ella; you need help.'

'You made me sick. You killed my parents. You killed Ben. Now this is your last chance. Tell me.'

'What do you want me to say? I did it to get my hands on the business? I did it because I always hated Mark? What? If it makes you happy, choose a reason and I'll admit to it.'

'I just want the truth!'

'You don't! I've told you the truth. You want me to lie to you, so tell me, just tell me the lie, and I'll admit to it.'

She shook her head, disgusted with him for exploiting the intensity of her feelings to convince her she'd been led astray. And that angered her almost more than his crime, that he was denying her any kind of explanation. Even now, he was trying to play the innocent and cast her as the villain.

She wasn't sure how long she'd been silent when she heard him speak again.

'Ella, I know you're confused, but I'm asking you, just for one moment, to ignore everything you've heard or been told, everything you've imagined. Forget all of it. Just . . . Just look into your heart.'

Her heart. What did he know of her heart?

She turned to Dan and said, 'Kill the kids.' Lucy produced a muffled scream and Simon started to beg; she could hear her name being repeated, more desperate each time.

She concentrated her attention on Dan but he looked troubled, as though he hadn't heard her properly, sounding apologetic as he finally said, 'I don't do kids.'

Ella was thrown by the comment, saying, 'Why not?'

'Nobody ever asked me. You know it isn't right; they're kids.'

She looked at them. The last time she'd seen them she'd loved them but she didn't anymore, and not because of anything they'd done, but because her capacity to love anyone had been slowly crushed and was gone.

She had to kill them. If she let them live, then one day they'd no longer be innocents but people like her, seeking to avenge the deaths of their parents. And she wanted to kill them for the pain their deaths would inflict on Simon in the final few minutes of his life. That was her vengeance, to return that pain to him.

'Okay, take all their gags off.' She reached out and took the gun off him again, and he walked over and removed the gags. There was too much noise then and not enough air—the kids' crying and Lucy's desperate pleas added to Simon's.

Dan came back over and said, 'What now?'

She looked at Simon as she said, 'This is for Ben.' She lifted the gun, deaf to the pleas. She found Harry first, let his face slip out of focus beyond the end of the barrel, pulled the trigger.

Even with the silencer, the shot was loud enough to cause a momentary hiatus. It was broken by Simon's animal wail, George's high-pitched scream. She looked at Lucy but she'd fainted, lying slumped back on the seat now. Harry had been thrown onto the floor; she'd been aiming for his forehead but had hit his face and left it unrecognizable with chopped blood.

Without giving herself time to think she turned her aim on George and fired again. There was no hiatus this time, just the summary silencing of his terrified scream. She fired another shot at Lucy where she lay unconscious but missed, hitting the seat. On the second attempt she put a bullet right into the side of her head.

Simon's wail descended slowly into a punch-drunk silence. She surveyed the wreckage—Lucy, the children's bodies, their thin little legs sticking out of knee-length shorts, matching shirts because they'd been coming to dinner.

She'd lost all sense of Dan still being there but then she heard him speak.

'Bloody hell! Why did you have to go and do that, Ella?'

She looked at him, his expression one of total bafflement, and scorn perhaps, and she said, 'It was the least I could do.' She turned back to Simon and said, 'Look at your children, Simon, look at your wife. You did this to them. Innocent children, and you killed them just like you killed Ben, his whole life still ahead of him.'

He didn't look at them, making eye contact with her instead, fixing her, unblinking. She was expecting him to say something, to abuse her, throw curses, but he remained silent, a lack of response that unnerved her.

'Well, don't you have anything to say for yourself?' He still didn't speak and it angered her. He didn't deserve this now, to suddenly adopt a mantle of dignified silence. It wasn't his right. She lifted the gun and shot at his body, the bullet hitting the side of his stomach, the blood soaking quickly into his shirt. Simon didn't flinch, though, as though he hadn't even felt it and wasn't aware of the wound.

He continued to stare at her in silence. It crossed her mind that it wasn't intentional, that he was simply too traumatized to say anything, but looking into his eyes, she knew that he was defying her, denying her the satisfaction of seeing him broken.

'No last words at all?' Nothing. There was a stillness and remoteness about him that infuriated her. Her arm felt tired but she lifted it one more time and shot him in the head, a good shot, the blood spurting out of him.

Fatigued, she held out the gun to Dan. The scene in front of her made no visual sense. Her feelings were confused, too, a strange mix of completeness and emptiness.

She produced a weak smile for Dan. He was staring down at George and Harry, though, and when he finally met her gaze all he could do was shake his head, his eyes swimming with a dulled contempt.

She couldn't understand it. People like him and Lucas killed for money. They killed good and bad, guilty and innocent, offering no mercy to their victims. Who were they to think ill of her, to condemn what she'd done?

Dan was sickened because she'd refused to spare even the children, but that choice hadn't been hers; it had been made for her by Simon. She'd returned to Simon what he'd so cruelly handed to her. She'd done unspeakable things but they'd been right. And she didn't care whether Dan could see that or not; she knew it to be true.

Chapter Twenty

He should have brought his own car. The heater wasn't working in the rental car, which hadn't been a problem the previous day, but today was much colder. Even his feet were cold. He'd have found it amusing if he didn't feel so completely ridiculous.

It wasn't much of a walk between here and the rue Saint Benoit, but the idea was that the rental car could act as a blind, which would be less conspicuous than simply standing across the street from the house. That was the idea, anyway, but the rental car was freezing.

He got out and started to walk, heading for the cafe that he now knew was a frequent haunt of hers. He'd wait in there; if she showed, all well and good. If she didn't, at least he'd be warm.

The car acted as a barrier to the truth. For the most part, as he sat there, he could fool himself that he was on just another job. Out on the street, though, walking past the house, he felt ill at ease in his own skin, full of self-doubt.

It was a feeling he carried with him into the cafe and he sat dwelling on it as he waited for his coffee. At home, in isolation, he convinced himself that he was ready to come back out into the world, but every time he ventured out, it was as if he'd made no progress at all.

What had really changed since his previous visit when Madeleine had pleaded with him to stay away? He'd turned his back on his old life again, retreated from the world again. This time he was certain he was done with it, but then he'd felt like that before, so how certain could he be? How certain could he ever be that there wouldn't be another phone call that he'd feel obliged to respond to?

By the time he'd finished his second cup of coffee, he was close to giving up, not just on the cafe, on this cold January day, but on the whole thing. He still didn't think he had the courage to speak to her or face Madeleine again, so maybe it was better just to go and wait for her to find him if ever she wanted to.

Then she came in, alone this time, and he was captivated all over again. He panicked when he realized he hadn't brought his newspaper. He considered getting up to take one of the cafe's papers but he didn't want to draw attention to himself.

The young waiter came over to chat, helping her with her coat and scarf. She was wearing a red sweater, a color that suited her like it suited her mother. She didn't appear to order anything and he was curious to see who she was meeting.

For ten minutes, he was happy just watching her. He could have sat looking at her all day. He only wished that she would see him, too, but the couple of times she looked in his direction she appeared not to notice him at all. Then, after ten minutes, she checked her watch and reached into her coat pocket for a phone.

At first, he couldn't hear her speaking but she became angrier as the brief conversation ran its course and the final few words of the call carried across to him. It bothered him that she was angry, that someone had stood her up.

She grabbed her coat and got up to leave. Without even thinking about it, Lucas stood too and then didn't know why except he was fired up with adrenaline. He went to sit down again but realized that for the first time she was looking at him, probably curious at the way he'd responded so directly to her movements.

He'd always felt with a hit that there was one moment when everything was right for doing the job perfectly, and that unless that moment was seized it would turn messy—still feasible, but messy. This wasn't a hit, but this was that moment.

He took a step towards her, going through the words in his head, trying to imagine himself saying them. She didn't move, just kept her ground, staring at him with the same look of expectancy and curiosity.

He smiled apologetically and, painfully slowly, he said, '*Excusez moi, mademoiselle, vous ne me connaissez pas, mais, uh, je suis . . .*' He was grinding the words out one by one.

'It's okay. I speak English.' Her accent was flawless. She appeared to register his shock but couldn't know why he was surprised. 'And I know who you are, I think.'

'You do?' She took her eyes off him for the first time now, looking around to see if they were attracting attention standing there.

'Would you like to sit down?' He nodded but it wasn't so much an invitation as a request for some discretion. As soon as they were sitting, the waiter came over and she ordered in French before saying to him, 'What would you like?'

'Coffee, please. Decaf if they have it.' He felt like he could do without any more caffeine; two coffees down and his heart was running at a canter.

She gave the order, then said, 'You're my father?' Her tone was businesslike, a clarification, a coolness in her voice that gave him a bad feeling.

'Yes, I am.'

'Why didn't you come sooner? I'm fourteen now.'

'Two reasons.' He paused for a second. He'd thought about this meeting so many times and yet still found himself uncertain about how to put the failings of his life into words. 'I loved Madeleine, so much that I didn't want her to know who I really was. When she became pregnant, that changed everything; I had to tell her. She ended the relationship, and we agreed it was best for you that I wasn't around. My life was, uh . . .'

'She said you were a criminal.'

He was hurt that Madeleine had described him like that and yet she'd been right. He'd never been to prison, never been troubled by the police, but he was a criminal. He couldn't even claim the dubious justification of having worked for governments; the people he'd worked for had paid more and asked for worse than any government agency would ever have done.

'Yes, until maybe four years ago, I was a criminal.' He felt like a liar. The work for Mark Hatto didn't trouble him, even killing to keep Ella alive. But what he'd done for her—killing Novakovic, leading her to Bruno—that had been too close to his old life, close enough for him to feel guilty for not mentioning it, for not admitting that those four years had culminated in one bloody fall from grace.

'You said there were two reasons.'

He nodded.

'I was scared.'

She looked skeptical and said, 'Of a little girl?' She was teasing him, with a slight smile that encouraged him. He had been scared, though—so scared of loss that he'd preferred to make himself invulnerable in the first place by always keeping life at arm's length.

The waiter brought his coffee, hot chocolate for Isabelle. Lucas could see him smiling slyly at her, as if making clear that he'd want an explanation at some later date. She dipped a finger in her drink and tasted it and then said, 'Why did you stop being a criminal?'

He found the word grating now but certainly didn't want to have to explain the exact nature of the things he'd done.

'Partly because I could. Partly so I could sit here one day and tell you I'd given up.'

She smiled, her first real smile since he'd sat down, and said, 'You thought about me?'

'Not at first. The last four or five years, though, more and more, every time I saw a kid I thought might be your age. I'd never seen a picture, didn't know your name. I came here last summer but . . .'

'She told me you came. We had a fight.' As an afterthought, she added, 'Nothing serious.'

He smiled, pleased that she'd fought with Madeleine for sending him away, even if she dismissed it now.

'You look just like her. I'd been worrying that I wouldn't recognize you but I knew the second I saw you. Short hair but otherwise you could be her double.'

'My eyes are blue, like yours.' No sooner had she said it than she looked over his shoulder and said, 'Excuse me.' She got up, looking ruffled.

Lucas turned in his seat and followed her progress to the door of the cafe, where she intercepted a boy. It looked like one of the boys he'd seen her with the previous summer but he couldn't be sure.

Isabelle had her back to Lucas and as she talked; the boy looked mischievously over her shoulder, trying to get a good look at him. He wondered if this was who she'd planned to meet and what she was saying to him now.

When she came back, she said, 'I'm sorry.'

'Was that who you were waiting for?'

'Yes. And no, he isn't. We're friends.' He smiled at her defensiveness and neither of them said anything for a moment, a pause that seemed to embarrass her. 'So, what do you want to know about my life?'

He sipped at his coffee, which he guessed *was* a decaf because it tasted much worse than the others had, and then he said, 'I already know a little. I know you have a brother now. I saw him last summer.'

She smiled. 'Isn't he adorable? Louis. He's five years old.'

'Louis. After your grandfather.'

She looked surprised, saying, 'You know my grandparents?'

'I met them a few times. I liked them. Are they still alive?'

'Yes, of course.' She looked suddenly intrigued and said, 'What about my other grandparents?'

'They died a long time ago. I don't even remember them.'

'Oh. Do you have brothers or sisters?'

He shook his head, feeling like a disappointment. For years, she'd probably imagined this whole other side to her family and now she was faced with the stark truth, that he brought only himself, half a person.

'And Louis' father?'

The question appeared to sadden her and for a moment his imagination started building visions of an unhappy relationship between them, but then she said, 'He died too, three years ago. An accident driving his car.'

Lucas was annoyed with himself because his first instinct was to be happy, relieved that this man was dead. It made no difference to him because he knew Madeleine wouldn't let him back into her life, but it still made him happy to know that no other man was there.

He realized then, though, how saddened Isabelle was just in mentioning it and he felt sad for her, and for Louis, who'd come to the door last summer to see who was there. And he was sad for Madeleine, because she deserved to be happy but had been poorly treated instead, by him first and then by fate.

She recovered herself now and said, 'We shouldn't talk about sad things today. Do you live in England?'

'No, Switzerland.'

She laughed and said, 'But your French isn't very good!'

'That's true. I live in a German-speaking area.'

'You speak German?'

'No.' She laughed loud enough this time for a couple of people to look over and smile at her.

'I could teach you French. Some German too. Can you ski, where you live?'

'Yes, good skiing. I hope you'll come one day.'

'I hope so too.' He smiled. He wanted to stand up and tell the whole cafe in his hopeless French that this was his daughter. It was enough for him just to be with her, though, and for her not to hate him.

He walked back with her, both of them coming to a halt before they reached the house.

'I'll be in Paris for a few more days at least. Maybe we can meet again.'

'Of course, we must. I'm happy you came.'

'Me too. And I'm sorry for . . .' What was he sorry for? For not being around, for being the person he'd been? 'I'm just sorry.'

'It's the past,' she said, a protective lie.

She seemed to hesitate, unsure of herself, and then she hugged him. He panicked briefly, thinking she'd feel the gun through his clothes, but with a strange feeling of lightness, of being suddenly unburdened, he remembered that he wasn't carrying one.

He watched her walk away and as she neared the house he crossed the street and collapsed into the driver's seat of his car as he finally allowed it all to sink in. He couldn't recall the last time he'd been this happy, a deep-seated euphoria that made him want to scream, that filled him with energy and left his hands trembling.

He sat there for a couple of minutes, unable to do anything, traumatized by the happiness of finding her.

Then from the corner of his eye he noticed movement at the door of the house. Before he'd even registered her, Madeleine had covered a good part of the ground between them, her face burning with anger. She was wearing pale, fitted trousers, a clingy sweater, and even as he braced himself he was amazed again at how she'd kept her figure.

She got into the passenger seat and slammed the door shut. She didn't say anything at first and he turned to look at her. He knew she'd aged in fifteen years, but he couldn't see it; she looked as beautiful as the first time he'd seen her.

'You promised,' she said, still looking straight ahead.

'Well, I was wrong. I should have stayed.'

She turned to face him. 'That choice wasn't yours. What kind of life would we have had, Luke? You, a murderer, consorting with murderers. How can you even have the audacity to come here now, to expose her to that?'

'I haven't exposed her to anything. I left all that behind a long time ago.'

'And how do you know it won't come back?'

'I just know. It isn't an issue.'

'It is an issue! You're a murderer—that doesn't go away.'

'Doesn't it? Not ever? I'll always be a murderer and she'll always be the child of a murderer. Is that it?'

'The world you inhabit . . .'

He cut her off, saying, 'I told you, I'm finished. I'm out. You have to believe me, Madeleine.' She didn't respond and a second later he said, 'Do you honestly think I'd have come here if there was any risk to either of you?'

She threw her arms up, exasperated, and said, 'I don't know what to do! The genie is out of the bottle. If I forbid her now it makes me look like a bad parent. Me! Could you not have waited a few more years?' He didn't answer, because it hardly seemed necessary. He'd waited too long already. She didn't say anything for a short while and then said, 'I propose a cooling-off period, give her time to think about this. If she still wants to see you, we'll have to make arrangements. It can be done through our lawyers.'

'Lawyers! What need have we of lawyers? Surely after all this time we can speak face to face.'

'No. Perhaps Isabelle wants you to become part of her life, but I don't want you to become a part of mine. Is it too much, to ask you to stay away?'

'Yes, it is.' She looked at him, surprised because he'd given the wrong answer, one he wasn't qualified to give. 'Maybe I shut it out because I thought you had a husband. I wouldn't have interfered, and I'm sorry about what happened to him but, Madeleine, I didn't just come back here for Isabelle.'

She looked at him askance and said, 'How very presumptuous of you.' She looked sad as she added, 'I loved Laurent very much. We miss him terribly.'

'Then you should understand how I feel.'

'Oh, please don't!'

'Why not? I'm not throwing you a line. I don't even have the . . .' Whatever it was he didn't have, he couldn't even think of the word for it. 'You're the only person I ever loved, and you're the only person who ever loved me. I don't expect it to mean anything to you—why should it? But it's true.'

She smiled a little, and looked almost touched as she said, 'It means something, and I did love you. It's how I managed to hate you for so long, for the truth of who you were. That was the truth—who you were.'

'Who I *was*,' he said, stressing the past tense. 'And do you still hate me now?' She sighed, a sigh that seemed to suggest there was no point anymore, that too much life had happened to her. He wanted to comfort her, put his hand on her shoulder, but he restrained himself and said, 'Then could we be friends? That's all I want—to be able to talk to you, be in the same room. God, just to be in the same room as you! To be friends.'

She shook her head for a few seconds, thinking, locked in some internal dialogue, and said finally, 'I'll never fall in love with you again. You understand that?'

'I know.'

She still couldn't bring herself to give her assent, saying instead, 'Where are you living now?'

'Switzerland.' She laughed. 'What?'

'Your whole life, you choose to live in places where they don't speak English.'

'I like having a reason not to talk.' She laughed again, more of a politeness, an awkwardness that was like a first meeting. She brushed a strand of hair from her face and he noticed the wedding ring. 'What about you? These last few years must have been tough.'

'Oh, you know.' She looked at the dashboard and said, 'Would you turn on the heater? It's very cold.'

'It doesn't work. Rental car—I should have taken it back.'

She looked at the heater like she was annoyed with it, then stared at him, fixing her eyes on his, an air of deliberation about her that put him on edge because he knew what she was thinking.

'Luke, I won't ask for more promises, but I couldn't bear for the children to be hurt again. I couldn't . . .' He put his hand up, putting his fingers over her lips, stopping her words and fears, the touch of her mouth careering through his nervous system like it was wired directly into the past, bypassing everything that had come between. He lowered his hand again and she closed her eyes, the deliberation still in progress. Finally she said, 'Okay, you can come in.' She still sounded unconvinced that she'd made the right decision, and maybe it would be a long time before she would be convinced.

They got out of the car and walked towards the house, back towards the only sense of home and family he'd ever known. He walked back from the wilderness with the woman he'd loved almost half his life. And he was happy, because as much as this was only a first step, he knew he'd never be alone again, that the person who'd so desperately sought such isolation had that morning finally ceased to exist, no less than if he'd died there.

Chapter Twenty-One

As he got closer he could see that his regular news vendor was back behind her stand. She saw him coming and waved, and he said, 'Where have you been, Wendy? My days haven't been the same.'

'Holiday,' said Wendy, smiling broadly, her teeth all over the place. 'The Canaries.'

'Very nice. I'll have a *Sydney Morning Herald*, please.'

She laughed loudly. It tickled him that the same joke always cracked her up like that.

'*Evening Standard* or nothing.'

'*Evening Standard* it is, then. What's the news?' She held the front page for him to see before she started reading, long enough for him to see the picture of Ella.

Slow and deliberate, Wendy said, 'Guide dogs, the homeless and terminal cancer patients will be among the many to benefit from one of the largest charitable bequests ever made. The will of the murdered heiress, Gabriella Hatto, has left her entire estate, thought to be worth hundreds of millions of pounds, to a variety of charities.' She looked from the paper and up at Dan as she said, 'What do you think of that?'

It wasn't clear whether she wanted a view on her reading of it or the actual story and he said, 'Pretty amazing. They know who did it yet?'

Wendy shrugged as if to suggest it had been a stupid question, saying then, 'Gotta be the uncle. I mean, where are they? Where have they gone? South America, you mark my words.' Somebody else leaned across to pick up a paper and she said, 'Okay, hold your horses.'

Dan gave her the money for the paper and said, 'See you tomorrow, Wendy.'

'And you, my love. Take care.' He walked on. She didn't know his name, and had never seemed curious. He only knew hers because she had a habit occasionally of talking about herself in the third person.

He walked back to the flat and opened the paper out on the kitchen table, pages four and five where the full story was repeated across the double spread, together with a photo montage illustrating the charities that would benefit from her money.

It was a shame, really, because he'd liked her, and she'd been a nice-looking girl, too. But he'd done the right thing; there was no doubt in his mind about that. He'd done for her what he would have done for a lame horse or any other wounded animal.

He'd even played devil's advocate with himself, asking who he was to decide that she'd no longer deserved to live. He hadn't judged her, though, nor had he condemned her. He'd simply seen the point she'd reached, beyond ever redeeming herself. Maybe she hadn't known it, but before Dan had ever met her she'd been fatally wounded; all he'd done had been to put her out of her misery.

The whole thing had been a weird business anyway. He'd given it a lot of thought, too, amazed at the way an entire family could have been destroyed like that, a destruction so comprehensive it was almost like someone had planned it that way.

Turning his mind to better things, he got up now and went over to the fridge, already excited about the meal he was making. He took out the duck breasts he'd marinated that morning, then methodically placed the other ingredients around them, everything within easy reach.

He opened the wine and poured himself a glass, then looked across the counter at an imaginary camera and said, 'Nice glass of Moore Farm Shiraz, and here are those duck breasts I prepared earlier.' He carried on talking through what he was about to do, thinking how there was probably a gap in the TV market for something like that.

He laughed then, thinking for some reason or other how one day there'd be a Mrs. Borowski. He didn't know what had brought it to mind but it was a nice thought. She was out there right now, probably, and she didn't know how lucky she was.

Acknowledgments

Thanks, as ever, to Deborah Schneider and the team at Gelfman Schneider/ICM. Thanks to Emilie Marneur, Alan Turkus and all at Thomas & Mercer. And finally, a nod to Rob and Lucia – Budapest, a long time ago!

About the Author

Kevin Wignall is a British writer, born in Brussels in 1967. He spent many years as an army child in different parts of Europe, and went on to study politics and international relations at Lancaster University. He became a full-time writer after the publication of his first book, *People Die* (2001). His other novels are *Among the Dead* (2002); *Who Is Conrad Hirst?* (2007), shortlisted for the Edgar Award and the Barry Award; and *Dark Flag* (2010). *The Hunter's Prayer* was originally titled *For the Dogs* in the USA. The film *The Hunter's Prayer*, directed by Jonathan Mostow and starring Sam Worthington and Odeya Rush, will be released worldwide in 2015.